A WEDDING FOR CHRISTMAS

MICHELE BROUDER

Editing by Jessica Peirce

Book Cover Design by Rebecca Ruger

A Wedding for Christmas

To God be the Glory.

CHAPTER ONE

October

Annie took a deep breath and stared at the front door of the Barnetts' brownstone. It was adorned with a luxurious wreath bedecked in autumn leaves. Over lunch the previous week, Carol Barnett had mentioned to Annie that she wanted her to meet someone her husband worked with. Conveniently, they all worked in the same building.

She didn't know why she had agreed to it and hoped she hadn't made a mistake in doing so. Blind dates, from what she'd heard, were notoriously risky and rarely worked out. She hadn't been on a date since Brad had dumped her over a year ago, and in fact she was still waiting for him to come to his senses. But at least this was something to do on a Sunday afternoon, she supposed. It got her out of her apartment, and there was something to be said for that.

In one hand she held a box of cupcakes from an upscale bakery in Manhattan, a bottle of wine in the other. She summoned her courage and pressed the bell. Deep in the interior of the brownstone, she heard the ringing, followed by footsteps that grew louder as they got closer.

She had not slept well the night before; she'd been nervous about the meeting. Absentmindedly, she ran her tongue across her top teeth. She blinked hard, hoping her mascara was still where it was supposed to be: on her eyelashes.

Carol's husband, Doug, answered the door. "Hey, Annie, it's great to see you!"

Annie stepped inside and hugged him in greeting. "How are you, Doug?"

"Great. Here, let me take your coat," Doug said.

The entryway was well-appointed, with a parquet floor, white walls, and a gold mirror over a console table. On top of the table was an arrangement of calla lilies in a crystal vase. Annie set the wine and the box of cupcakes down on the table, removed her coat, and handed it to Doug, who took it from her and hung it in the hall closet.

Carol emerged from the front room and broke into a smile at the sight of her friend. "Annie!" She enveloped her in a hug.

"I'll take these back to the kitchen," Doug said, picking up the cupcakes and wine and disappearing down the hallway.

Carol made a *tsk* sound and said to Annie, "You didn't have to bring anything."

Annie frowned. "But I wanted to." She smoothed down the front of her red dress. "Do I look all right?"

Carol smiled at her. "You look beautiful." Sensing Annie's nervousness, she reached out and touched her arm. "Relax. Oliver is here and he's very nice. Doug and I think you two would be perfect together."

That's what Carol had said during the week. Annie had to admit to a certain bit of curiosity; what kind of man did Doug and Carol think would be perfect for her? She touched her earring and followed Carol into the front room. There, at the white marble fireplace, stood a man with his back to them, studying a framed photo he held in his hand.

From the back, he looked good, Annie thought. Tall, maybe just over six feet, with broad shoulders and thick auburn hair. He set the frame back down on the mantel and turned around at the sound of their entrance.

Annie's mouth opened slightly. He was quite handsome. Carol had never said anything about his good looks. A bracket of dimples framed his smile. But it was his eyes that caught her attention. They were the color of rich coffee and reminded her of lazy Sunday mornings spent reading in bed. He was the whole package, and Annie didn't know quite what to do with it. She smiled back, enjoying the look of him and all the possibilities he presented.

"Oliver, I'd like to introduce you to Annie Beasley. We work together," Carol said.

Oliver stepped forward, extending his hand. "Oliver Chesterfield."

At the sound of his polished British accent, Annie practically sighed.

"Hi" was all she could squeak out.

When he took her hand in his, the contact made the hairs stand up on her arm. His eyebrows raised ever so slightly and she couldn't help but wonder if he had felt it, too. He smiled, and something passed between them, she was sure of it.

"I've been anxious to meet you, Annie," he said.

Doug entered the room with some wine. Annie refused, wanting to be in full control of her faculties. Within a few minutes of meeting Oliver, she found many things about him that intrigued her, and she wanted to make a good impression. She was glad she'd chosen the red dress.

"Annie moved here from Hope Springs back in February," Carol offered.

"Does it spring eternal?" Oliver cracked.

Annie frowned in confusion, her mind going blank.

"The proverb?" he prompted.

"Oh right," Annie said. She giggled. *No! Don't start giggling.*

Before she could answer his original question, he asked, "And where's Hope Springs?"

Annie nodded, trying to get her bearings. Her palms had gone damp. She bit her lip and reminded herself not to say too much. "Middle of the state. Middle of nowhere, actually."

"Why did you move to New York?" he asked.

Annie shrugged, her eyes wide. "I don't know, seemed the thing to do. I'm normally not so impulsive, but this was a spur-of-the-moment decision." She managed to refrain from volunteering the history behind that decision, although she continued talking. "It's so different from my hometown. It's like day and night. The moon and the sun. I feel like the country mouse who went to the city." She giggled some more.

Oliver's eyebrows knitted together ever so slightly, but enough for Annie to notice. She ran a hand through her hair.

"Oliver moved here last January," Doug informed her.

"Really? How exciting. How do you like it? It must be so different from England. Are you here permanently, or is it just a drive-by?" Annie asked, horrified. It was as if her tongue had a life of its own. Words and sentences were backing up in the queue and piling up on top of each other to get out of her mouth. She smiled so broadly that her cheeks began to hurt.

"I like it very much. I plan to stay here for the immediate future," he replied quietly.

"Maybe we'll have to do something to convince you to stay here permanently," Annie said. Her laughter had taken on a higher-than-normal pitch. Had she just said that? Behind her pasted-on smile, she cringed. *Calm down.*

But some internal force spurred her on. "There's so much to do and see in New York! Baseball, Broadway, the Statue of Liberty . . ." And on she went, her hand waving frantically like an aircraft marshaller directing a plane from the gate to the runway.

Carol and Doug exchanged a look. They'd never seen Annie like this. It was as if she were being controlled by some unseen entity.

"Where are you from?" Annie continued. "In England, I mean. I know you're from England, but where?" Another giggle escaped her lips.

"Somerset," he said. He was no longer smiling.

Annie shouldn't be smiling either. This was beginning to feel like that moment when the iceberg ripped through the side of the *Titanic*.

By the time they sat down for a dinner of Sunday roast, Annie felt slightly sick to her stomach with nerves. Throughout the meal, she was animated and talked nonstop, no longer listening to the conversation but instead, just waiting for her turn to say the next thing that popped into her head.

Oliver was quiet and offered one-word replies. Annie hoped that wasn't his personality. Carol looked at her pointedly, and normally, Annie would take the hint, but she just kept talking. She couldn't help it. The quieter Oliver became, the chattier she became. It was as if her motto was *Those silent spaces need to be filled*.

By the end of the meal, Annie had a headache. She needed a nap.

"Annie, would you mind helping me get the coffee and dessert ready?" Carol asked with a nod as she stood up and began clearing plates.

"Sure," Annie said, jumping up from her chair. Relief flooded her at the offer to leave the room. She'd wash the dishes by hand if it took her away from the table. And Oliver, who now seemed to regard her as if she had the plague.

Once in the kitchen, Carol set the plates down on the island and turned to Annie. "You're so nervous! But you don't have to be, it's all right," she said reassuringly.

"Maybe this wasn't a good idea," Annie said. She just wanted to go home.

"It can still be salvaged," Carol said.

Salvaged? Had it been that bad? Annie tried not to break out in a cold sweat.

"Can you pop back and ask Oliver if he'd like tea or coffee?" Carol said. At the sink, she filled the glass coffeepot with water.

Annie pushed through the butler door that led to the dining room and saw Oliver with his head in his hands as Doug asked, "What do you think?"

Oliver shook his head. "I'm afraid she's not for me. Certainly pretty, but way too much laughing and talking."

And that was that. Annie stood there, her face burning with embarrassment. Not wanting to be enlightened any further, she cleared her throat.

Doug looked up, aghast. "Annie!"

Oliver's head snapped up. He paled.

Annie forced a bright smile and spoke firmly. "Oliver, Carol wanted to know if you'd like coffee or tea?"

Oliver opened his mouth and stared at her for a minute before shaking his head. "Coffee is fine, thank you."

Annie returned to the kitchen, feeling a change come over her. "Oliver will have coffee," she told Carol.

Carol nodded, then frowned. "Are you all right? You're flushed."

Annie shrugged and smiled politely. "I'm fine." Suddenly she no longer felt nervous or giggly. It was amazing how you could pull yourself together when you no longer found someone attractive. Or they you.

Once the dessert and coffee were served, Annie rejoined the dinner table, sitting across from Oliver, her posture rigid against the back of her chair. She spoke when someone asked her a question, smiled politely, and might have even nodded a few times. The dessert and coffee were delicious, but she'd lost her appetite and after a few bites, she pushed her plate away. She did not look at Oliver. Doug, acutely aware of what had transpired, introduced one topic after another to keep the conversation going, but he was like a man trying to row a boat with one oar.

"Annie, where in New York do you live?" Oliver asked.

Annie looked at him. He shifted in his seat. Was he uncomfortable? Good, she thought.

"Brooklyn," Annie answered.

"There's a little Italian café there called Di Rossi's. The food is fabulous," Oliver said.

Annie was aware of it. It was within walking distance of her apartment, but she had never been there.

"What about Eckert's? It's mainly farm-to-table fare but it is also noteworthy," Oliver said.

"Nope," she replied. He didn't even live in Brooklyn and he had seen more of it than she had.

She sipped her coffee and cast a glance in Carol's direction. Carol frowned at her, not understanding. Annie gave her a small smile.

"Do you like living in the city?" Oliver pressed.

"Yes," she lied.

Now he was going to engage in conversation with her? Because he felt guilty? Just to make himself feel better? Annie's shoulders sagged and her energy seeped out of her. She finished the rest of her coffee in one gulp. It was time to go home.

Abruptly, she stood up and laid her napkin on the table. "I've got to go. Carol and Doug, I want to thank you for a lovely dinner. Oliver, it was nice meeting you."

Carol and Doug protested that she shouldn't leave and Oliver sat there, staring at the table.

But Annie was already walking toward the front hall with the intent to retrieve her coat from the closet. Doug reached her first.

"I'm sorry, Annie," he started.

"Why? You didn't do anything," Annie said.

Carol frowned at her husband, who said to her, "I'll tell you later."

Once she belted her coat, Annie said goodbye and thanked them again. As she walked out the front door, she was aware of Oliver stepping into the hall.

The front door closed behind her. Annie let go of the breath she'd been holding, then pressed her lips together and headed toward her car, her pace clipped. This had been a stupid idea. She wasn't ready. She was not going to cry! Her car was in sight; the available spot on the street so close to Carol's house was the only thing that had gone right. She had just clicked her key fob when she heard steps running behind her. "Annie!"

She turned to see Oliver in his coat, running down the street after her. She so wished he hadn't. *Just let it go,* she thought. This was only going to make it more painful than it already was.

The air was brisk and a cold breeze lifted her hair off her collar.

When Oliver reached her, he was slightly out of breath, his hair all over the place. Despite this, he was still quite handsome.

Annie remained silent.

He put up his hand. "Annie, I wanted to say I'm sorry. My manners were appalling."

"Yes, they were," she agreed. "Apology accepted. Goodbye." She hopped off the curb and got into her car without looking at him. He was still on the sidewalk when she pulled away. As much as she wanted to resist, she glanced back at him in the rearview mirror, still standing there.

That was it. No more blind dates. And no more handsome men. She'd have better luck with a troll.

That's what she got for daring to venture out of her apartment. For daring to try something new. For daring to try and move on from Brad.

Chapter Two

Thanksgiving

It was to be a small family gathering for Thanksgiving this year at Annie's parents' house. Usually, they'd have a houseful. Her parents, especially her mother, liked a party. But it was just Annie, her parents, Grandma Fischer and Grandpa Beasley, who both lived with her parents. Her sister was spending the holiday with her boyfriend's family. And this year Uncle Al, Aunt Betty, and Cousin Violet had decided to eat out for something different.

The smells of turkey and stuffing and apple pie filled the house, and Annie's stomach growled in response. She helped her mother in the kitchen.

"Mom, did you really need a twenty-pound turkey?" Annie said as her mother pulled the roasting tray out of the oven.

Peggy Beasley lifted the tented foil, filled the baster with drippings, and poured it over the turkey.

"For leftovers. Everyone loves a nice turkey sandwich the day after Thanksgiving."

She handed the oven mitts to her husband, Malcolm, who removed the bird from the oven and set it on the counter.

Annie set about mashing the potatoes with the electric mixer. She added a little bit of butter and warmed milk. The three of them managed to carry the dishes into the dining room.

Grandma Fischer and Grandpa Beasley were already seated at the table.

The dining room was one of Annie's favorite rooms in the house with its dark, heavy woodwork and coving, the old-fashioned wallpaper covered with birds and flowers, and the antique dining-room set that had belonged to Grandma Fischer's mother. Many happy gatherings had been held in this room. Above the walnut buffet hung a large artificial wreath, in the center of which stood a caroling Victorian couple with lighted candles. It was the only Christmas decoration up at present, but Annie knew that as soon as Thanksgiving dinner was over, her mother would start setting up her extensive Christmas collection.

"I'm starving," Grandma Fischer said. She set her electronic cigarette down on the table next to her knife.

Peggy looked around the table at the empty chairs. "It's a shame there's so few here this year."

"You've got me and Frieda." Grandpa Beasley smiled at her. "What more do you need?"

Annie laughed as she set down the sweet-potato casserole, its marshmallow topping baked to a golden brown. But she couldn't agree more with her grandfather. The current situation suited her perfectly.

Rachel had gone to Brian's this year for the holiday, and Annie was more than happy about that. Brian was Brad's younger brother, and he and Rachel had started dating right after she and Brad had broken up. At the time, Annie didn't think it would amount to much, but they'd been together now for more than a year. If Rachel married him, chances were Annie would be running into Brad at various family functions. She shuddered at the thought. Just because she was still in love with him didn't mean she wanted to see him. And still being in love with him put her at a distinct disadvantage. But she was getting ahead of herself. There had been no mention of a possible engagement.

Annie's mother ran back into the kitchen to get the gravy. Her father opened the top drawer of the buffet and removed the electric knife, and Annie took a seat at the table, across from her grandparents.

"How's the city?" Grandpa Beasley asked.

"Great, exciting," she answered over the whirr of the electric knife as her father, standing at the head of the table, started to slice the breast of the bird. Her mother set the gravy boat on the table, mumbled something about forgetting the cranberry sauce, and returned to the kitchen.

Annie helped herself to mashed potatoes, trying to muster an enthusiasm for her new home that she did not feel. She handed the bowl to her grandmother, who passed her the stuffing in return. They all looked at her as if they were expecting to be regaled with tales of the city.

"I went to a little Italian restaurant near me," she said. "It's a walk-down, in a basement."

"Eating in a basement! Ugh," Grandma said. "What your generation will do for fun. Basements are nothing more than a storage space for things you don't mind getting musty."

"Even so, it was delicious. Then there's this other restaurant, farm-to-table fare. It's a must-see place. Very nice." She hadn't been to any of these places but she hoped to someday. They didn't need to know that.

Her mother returned, still mumbling to herself as she set down the glass dish of cranberry sauce. Her gaze traveled the length of the table.

"Mom, sit down, we've got everything," Annie said.

Her mother hesitated and her father added, "Peggy, everything is fine. You've cooked the turkey beautifully."

Peggy nodded, satisfied, and turned to Annie. "Who did you go with to these restaurants?" she asked, taking her seat to the right of her husband.

"Just some friends from work," Annie fibbed.

"Well, I'm glad to hear you're getting out of that apartment," her mother said.

"You couldn't pay me enough to live in the city," Grandma said.

"The city pays us to keep you out," Grandpa quipped.

Grandma rolled her eyes, then asked, "What do you do on the weekends, Annie?"

Annie decided vague was best. "The usual. Hang out with friends. We usually go out for brunch on Sundays. Explore New York." Those were the things she *should* be doing.

"When are you coming back to Hope Springs?"

Annie shrugged, pouring gravy over her potatoes. "I'm not ready yet." The truth was, a part of her was more than ready to return to all that was familiar in her hometown. She just wasn't ready to admit defeat. She added, "Besides, I love my job." That much was true.

"And she's having too much fun!" Grandpa declared. "Leave her be."

Annie smiled. "That's exactly it, Grandpa." A little fib wouldn't hurt. She didn't want them to worry about her. They'd done enough of that in the past.

Peggy smiled at her husband and laid a hand on his.

"What time was Brian's mother having dinner?" Annie asked. She had spent a couple of Thanksgivings with Brad and Brian's family. They were nice people. Now, Rachel had slotted into her former role.

"They were eating at two," Peggy said.

"Oh, that's too early," Grandma said with a scowl. "That's right in the middle of nap time. No, that wouldn't suit me at all."

Annie suppressed a grin. A lot of things in this house were done to accommodate her grandmother. She knew her mother would have preferred to have an earlier dinner so she could have the rest of the day for herself.

"Are you going shopping tomorrow, Mom?"

"Oh no, you'd have to whip a horse," Peggy said with a shudder.

Grandma's lips stretched thin and she corrected, "You mean they'd have to horsewhip you."

Annie had given up a long time ago on correcting her mother. Peggy Beasley was known for mangling words, expressions, and phrases. They'd all made peace with it. All except Grandma.

"It seems to be serious between Rachel and Brian," Grandma said, her eyes not leaving Annie's face.

Annie lowered her head and studied her Thanksgiving meal. All the regulars were there on her plate and there was comfort in that, in tradition.

"It would seem so," Peggy said. "They sure do spend a lot of time together."

"They're young and they're in love," Malcolm said, helping himself to cranberry sauce.

Grandma harrumphed.

"Frieda, have you ever been young *or* in love?" Grandpa asked.

Grandma's eyebrows knitted together as if she'd just been asked if she'd ever been to Mars.

Grandpa hooted. "Just as I thought."

The plates were cleared and they let the dinner digest as Annie helped her parents with the cleanup. As the coffee brewed, Annie carried out the pies to the dining room: pecan, apple, and pumpkin. Once they were ready, Annie and her parents rejoined the table.

"Do you know when you'll be coming home for Christmas?" her mother asked.

"Not yet, it depends on when I get all my projects completed," Annie informed her. She was looking forward to coming home for Christmas. To her, being with family was what the holiday was all about.

As they ate pie and drank coffee, there was a commotion in the kitchen. They heard voices. Peggy had just stood up to investigate when Rachel burst through the door, followed by Brian. Her smile was wide and her eyes glittered.

"We're engaged!"

Everyone stood up to congratulate them.

"Have you set a date yet?" Annie asked.

Rachel shook her head. "Not yet. Next year probably."

Annie let out a quiet sigh of relief. At least she wouldn't have to deal with Brad until then.

"And I want you to be my maid of honor," Rachel said. "That's the only thing I know for sure."

Annie threw her arms around her. "Of course, Rachel." She was genuinely happy for her sister, but a small part of her wondered if she herself would ever have that kind of news to deliver. She swallowed hard and forced those thoughts away, choosing instead to concentrate on Rachel's good news. No matter what, she wasn't going to spoil Rachel's happiness.

They all sat down again. More coffee was served. More pie was sliced. The excitement abated and talk turned back to Christmas.

"Maybe we could have the two families get together at Christmas," Peggy suggested brightly.

Annie looked on, horrified. She did not treasure the thought of spending Christmas with her ex-boyfriend. Because then he would know. Brad would know that she still had feelings for him. She caught her father's eye and he shrugged helplessly.

As her mother enthused about the two families celebrating Christmas together, Annie stayed quiet, biting her lip. Her mind began to whirl. She *didn't* necessarily have to come home for Christmas. She could stay in the city. It was only one day. There was always so much work to be done that it wouldn't be a lie to use that as an excuse.

By the time the dessert plates were cleared, Annie was feeling much better. As she loaded the dishwasher, she made her decision: she'd stay in the city. And although the idea of spending the holiday in her apartment—alone—did not hold a lot of appeal, the thought of being here at home with the possibility of running into Brad held even less. No, she wasn't ready to meet up with him. Not yet.

After dinner, they all sat around the dining room table, the coffee gone cold, as Rachel and Brian talked about when they'd like to get married. They seemed to be leaning toward the spring, and Annie liked that idea. It would give her enough time to get used to the idea that her ex-boyfriend was going to be part of the family, in a sense.

The idea of not coming home for Christmas was growing on her. Images of marathons of binge-worthy television shows, fluffy robes, hot chocolate, and holiday cookies filled her head. She was practically smiling about it.

Rachel and Brian helped Malcolm bring down the boxes of Christmas decorations from the attic. Annie helped her mother put up the ceramic village in the front hall. Grandma and Grandpa settled into their recliners in the living room.

Within hours, they'd transitioned from Thanksgiving dinner to preparing for Christmas.

Annie lay on the cold tile floor of the front hall to place fake snow on the bottom shelf of the console table. Her mother had pulled up a chair and was arranging some of the village pieces on the top.

"It must be upsetting for you that Rachel is marrying Brad's brother," her mother said, not looking at her. With a damp cloth, she wiped off the ceramic apothecary shop before placing it on the blanket of fake snow.

Annie stopped what she was doing and sat up, kind of surprised at her mother's statement. "Oh, no, not at all. Do I wish she had fallen in love with someone else? Sure," she said, "but Rachel's so happy that I'm delighted for her." Annie resumed laying out the blanket of glittery fake snow. "And luckily, Brian isn't Brad."

Her mother looked at her, studying her face. "It might be best to get the first meeting with Brad over with. And you can do that at Christmas so it doesn't cast a pall over the wedding."

"You're probably right," Annie agreed, although she had no intention of ruining her favorite holiday by meeting up with her ex.

"I think we'll loop the train around the houses on your shelf. What do you think?" Peggy asked.

"Sounds like a plan."

CHAPTER THREE

December

Annie glanced up at the clock on her office wall. It was almost quitting time. She looked at the project before her, open on a screen on her desktop. When she'd been offered the job with Mason & Hodges Translation Services, it had been a dream come true, combining her love of the German language and reading. Some days she still had to pinch herself, as she couldn't believe she was getting paid to do something she loved.

Currently, she was working on translating a thriller that had been riding the bestseller lists for weeks. Her job wasn't narrowly defined by translating the English word into the German one. It was much more than that. It was about nuance and emotion and skill. Simply being fluent in two languages did not make you a translator.

In many ways, the job had saved her from a downward spiral after her breakup with Brad. It had given her a sense of purpose and pointed her life in another direction. One she had not expected. And as much as she'd wanted to remain in Hope Springs, moving to the city had been worth it if only for the job.

"Annie?"

Annie looked up to see Lenore standing in the doorway. Like Annie, she was single, and of a similar age. Sometimes they ate lunch together in the firm's break room, when Annie could pull herself away from her desk.

"Hi, Lenore."

"Look, we're getting together at my house tonight for our monthly book club meeting, and I wondered if you'd like to come over."

Annie hesitated. Lenore had asked her before, but Annie had always found an excuse. She might have moved away from Hope Springs, but she hadn't necessarily moved on from the life she'd had there.

"Ooh, I already have plans tonight," Annie lied. "Maybe next time."

"Yeah, sure, all right," Lenore said. But the expression on her face suggested she was skeptical.

Annie knew she should be carving out a new life for herself. Moving on with things. But that day was not today. And it probably was not tomorrow either.

Her cell phone rang, the vibration moving the phone along her desk. It was her mother.

"Hi, Mom," Annie said.

Mrs. Beasley went into a high-pitched stream of conversation. Annie frowned.

"Wait a minute, slow down. What about Rachel?" She thought her mother had just said that Rachel wanted to get married at Christmas.

"Rachel wants to have a Christmas wedding," her mother repeated, her voice an octave above its usual tone.

Annie glanced at her calendar, hopeful. "Next year, right?"

"Are you not listening?" her mother said, her voice full of exasperation. "This Christmas."

"This Christmas, as in this Christmas that's only weeks away?" Annie said.

"Yes, they've decided they don't want to wait and they're going to get married on Christmas Eve."

Annie leaned back in her chair, her shoulders sagging. This just couldn't be happening. She opted to be the voice of reason. "Christmas is busy enough, never mind throwing a wedding into the mix."

"I know it is, but we're all getting caught up in the brouhaha about it," her mother said.

Annie knew her mother meant *hoopla* but didn't bother correcting her.

"What about Dad?" she asked. Sometimes, her father was the only sensible one of the whole family.

"He's excited. You know we're not getting any younger, and we really would love some grandchildren," her mother said.

"Mom, try to talk some sense into her. She could have a nice wedding in January, a winter-wonderland kind of theme. Wouldn't that be better for everyone?" Annie almost cried into the phone.

"No, not January," her mother said. "The weather is too unpredictable."

Annie's mind scrambled for an excuse. She could say she had a non-refundable ticket for a cruise. But what would that say about her if she didn't want to go to her only sibling's wedding just because she wanted to avoid her ex-boyfriend?

She would have to go home to Hope Springs for Christmas.

"Where are they having it?" Annie asked, resigning herself to her fate.

"At the Bristol Manor."

Annie raised her eyebrows. "Nice."

Her mother chuckled. "It is but it isn't."

"Oh no, why?" Annie asked, afraid of the answer.

"The Bristol Manor is expensive. So, to cut corners, we're all going to pitch in and do everything else," her mother said.

"What?" Annie asked. "What do you mean?"

"For instance, we're going to do all the baking for the midnight tea-and-coffee service," her mother said.

"What else?" Annie asked.

"We're going to make the invitations online, and Rachel's friend from high school is going to do the flowers," her mother said.

"How many people is she inviting?"

"One hundred and fifty," her mother replied.

She could easily get lost in a crowd of one hundred and fifty people.

"Who's doing the catering?"

When her mother didn't say anything, Annie gripped the edge of her desk. She raised her voice slightly. "Please tell me we don't have to cook the dinners for over one hundred people!"

"Well, not exactly," her mother stammered.

Annie frowned and leaned forward in her office chair. "No, Mom. No. Don't tell me you're going to let Uncle Al and Aunt Betty do it."

"They offered, and we couldn't refuse," her mother explained.

"You just say no, that's it!" Annie cried.

Uncle Al and Aunt Betty's lifelong dream had been to run a business in the food service industry. They already had one failed catering business and one failed restaurant, which they blamed on the economy despite the fact that the economy was roaring at the time.

"She's my sister, and I want to help her," Peggy said.

"There's a difference between supporting someone and enabling them. They are not good cooks, you know that," Annie pointed out. "Cut the cord already."

"It's just the meal portion of the wedding," her mother said.

"How many times have you said that people going to a wedding and putting a lot of money into a card need a great meal? Huh?"

"I know what I said," her mother hissed and lowered her voice. "But they're offering to do it for free and I can hardly refuse."

Not my circus, not my monkeys, Annie told herself. "Okay, look, Mom, I've got to get back to work."

"Oh, wait, Annie, one more thing," her mother said. "I know it's a sensitive subject with Rachel marrying Brad's brother, but I hope you'll be able to enjoy yourself at this wedding."

That was easy for her to say. Annie would rather stick a hot poker in her eye than see her ex.

"And who knows, maybe the two of you could rekindle something," her mother said.

Annie paled and blurted, "There'll be no rekindling. Of anything. Besides, I'm dating someone."

"Oh, honey, that's wonderful! Will you bring him to the wedding?"

Before she could think, Annie said, "Yes. He'll probably come." She cringed. What had she just done?

"That's great news. You know, when you moved to the city, I was so worried about you," her mother admitted.

"You were?" Annie frowned. She never thought about her mother as worrying about her.

"I know how disappointed you were that your relationship with Brad ended, and I suppose you thought a change of scenery was needed, but I was so worried you'd just be working, with no personal life and no dating. And I was worried you'd become bitter."

"Ha!" Annie laughed. If her mother only knew what her life had turned into in the big city: work all day, bring some work home, and do some work on the weekends.

She blinked quickly and looked around her office for something to ground her.

"So, I can put you down for a one-plus on the guest list?" her mother asked.

Annie didn't hesitate. "Yes, I'm bringing a plus-one." There was no boyfriend, there weren't even prospects. But if there was one thing she was sure of, it was that she was bringing a date to her sister's wedding—she didn't care if she had to pay someone to do it.

On further consideration, a fake boyfriend might be just the thing to prove to Brad that she was no longer in love with him and that she had moved on. Without him.

CHAPTER FOUR

It wasn't his alarm that woke Oliver Chesterfield on the first Friday of December. It was his ringing phone. Rubbing his eyes, he glanced at the bedside clock and saw that it was only five-thirty. As he flipped on the bedside light, he yawned and picked up his phone. The name "Phillipa" flashed across his screen. He groaned. The fact that she was ringing him meant she wasn't on the plane that was due to land at JFK in four hours.

"Hello?"

"Oliver?"

"Phillipa, I'm here," Oliver said. "You're not on your plane."

"I waited until I thought you'd be up. Did I wake you?" she asked.

"No, I was just getting up," he lied. "What's wrong?"

"I'm sick. I've got sick coming out of every orifice," she explained.

Oliver winced. "Are you all right?"

"I'll be fine. Just didn't want to come over and spread around this kind of cheer. It's running out of me faster than—"

"I'm good, details not necessary."

Oliver and Phillipa had been best friends since they were young children. They'd grown up in the same village. And although nothing would make his mother happier than if he married Phillipa, Oliver didn't harbor those kinds of feelings for his friend. And she regarded him as a brother she liked to wind up regularly.

Phillipa laughed weakly on the other end of the line. "I know how squeamish you are. I must have eaten some dodgy curry."

"I'm not surprised, when you insist on buying food from the back of a truck instead of going into a perfectly good restaurant," Oliver said.

"They're called food trucks and they're all the rage. You should try one sometime. It might loosen you up," she suggested.

"Mmm," he said, deciding that it was too early for a conversation about the merits of food from a truck.

"Anyway, I'm sorry I won't be able to help you out," Phillipa said, referring to his holiday party later that evening.

"No worries," he said. No sense in making her feel guilty.

"How is it even possible that getting a promotion at your firm hinges on you having a girlfriend?" she asked again, as she had when he'd first asked her to accompany him. Phillipa had an art degree from the Sorbonne, her preferred medium being textiles. She despised conventions or restrictions of any kind.

"It's all about appearances," he said.

"Ugh," Phillipa pronounced.

The firm of Gilbert, Hardcastle, and Jones had been around for more than half a century. The only surviving founding member was Mr. Hardcastle. Although retired, he still made the trip down from his estate in Connecticut a couple of times a month to be a "presence." He talked often about his wife of fifty-five years, his six children and numerous grandchildren. He was a family man, and his firm was all about traditional values.

Phillipa continued speaking. "I don't know how you stand all that. Why can't you advance based solely on merit? Why is it so important for you to look like a family man?"

Oliver sighed. "I know, it's old-fashioned. And it is based on my merit, but this helps. Everyone vying for advancement at the firm has worked hard, and everyone will be doing whatever they can to get a promotion."

Now wasn't the time to get into a debate with her about his job and whether she thought it was worthy.

The only thing that mattered was that Oliver thought it was important. To him, it was.

They chatted for five more minutes before Phillipa announced that she had to get to a bathroom, and hung up.

After he disconnected, he sat for a minute before deciding he might as well get up. Going into work early would give him a head start on the day. And if by some miracle a date for his firm's Christmas party should happen to fall out of the sky, then it would justify leaving early in the evening.

Oliver cleared everything off his desk and glanced at his watch and then up at the great clock on the wall to confirm the time. Only three more hours until the party. He was not a nervous person by nature, but there was a certain amount of anxiety accompanying this event. Especially now that he was without a date.

It was his first Christmas party since he'd taken the position last January. He wasn't one for parties usually but this one was important, with Laurence Hardcastle there to shake hands and schmooze and make decisions as to who would be moving up in the ranks.

Oliver had been with the firm only a short time when they'd announced last year's new partners. There'd been champagne and a lot of back-slapping. Overall, it had been good fun.

Never one to brag, he'd thought his first year had gone swimmingly well. And he was hoping there would be a prize at the end of it: namely, a promotion.

He knew Mr. Hardcastle to be a stickler for details and a traditionalist to boot. But Oliver had not put a foot wrong since he'd arrived in New York eleven months ago. He'd been careful about that. If that made him boring, then so be it. Already around the office, he was known as being dedicated, even a workaholic. Case in point: he was still there at the office when he could have gone home. Most everyone had only worked half a day so they could spend time getting ready for the evening's events.

And after mulling over everything all morning, Oliver decided he did not need a date. He would simply explain that Phillipa had gotten sick and couldn't make it. Besides, Phillipa was right. It shouldn't matter whether he was married or in a committed relationship or not. His work ethic and his accomplishments should speak volumes. By midafternoon, he had what he was going to say to Mr. Hardcastle pretty well rehearsed.

Doug Barnett stuck his head in the doorway.

"You're still here?" he asked.

"Just tidying up my desk," Oliver answered.

"I thought you'd be home, mentally prepping for tonight," Doug joked.

Doug could joke about it; he'd made full partner last February.

"I'm good," Oliver said with a nod. He wasn't sure if the nod was to convince or reassure himself.

"Phillipa make it in all right?" Doug asked.

Oliver quickly explained the situation.

"That's too bad. Who's your backup?"

Oliver scowled. "Backup? No one. I'm going by myself." He thought of the tuxedo that was hanging at home on the outside of his wardrobe, ready for him to don.

Doug lifted his eyebrows and then sighed. He slumped into the chair in front of Oliver's desk. He rubbed his hand over his mouth and chin. "You couldn't get anyone else to go with you?"

"Who was I going to ask?" He looked through the glass wall of his office, which overlooked the interior of the firm. He hadn't wanted to ask any of the women he worked with. That wouldn't have worked for two reasons: first, it would be awkward come Monday morning. Second, Mr. Hardcastle frowned on workplace romance.

Doug shook his head and looked up toward the ceiling. "What am I going to do with you, Chesterfield?"

Oliver was confused. To him, everything was sorted out. He was going to explain it to Mr. Hardcastle. Plain and simple. Oliver told Doug this.

Doug shook his head. "You don't get it."

Oliver sighed; the topic of conversation was making him weary.

"Yes, you can explain to Old Man Hardcastle that your date bailed because she was sick," Doug explained. "But from where he's standing, you're from another country and it appears you're not setting down roots in New York. And that could be a liability."

"How?"

"You could decide at any point you might want to go back home. So why should he give you any kind of promotion?"

Oliver grimaced. He hadn't thought of it like that. Truthfully, he was in no hurry to go home. He'd grown to love New York. But there was nothing to demonstrate that to Mr. Hardcastle.

Oliver's brows knitted together in consternation. "I can hardly conjure up a date at this point."

Doug smirked. "Really? We're in a skyscraper full of single women. Your accent alone guarantees an immediate yes. I bet the first woman you see and ask, will say yes."

"I can't walk up to a stranger and ask her to a Christmas party that's happening in a few hours," Oliver said, appalled.

"Why not?" Doug asked. He stood up suddenly from his chair. "I'll be right back. I've got an idea."

"Wait—"

"Just keep an open mind," Doug said before he disappeared out the door.

Would Mr. Hardcastle hold it against him that he was single? Did Oliver want to wait another year or more to climb the corporate ladder? Especially when he'd worked so hard this past year. Ironically, he might have been able to find himself a girlfriend if he hadn't spent all his time at work. It was difficult when you worked twelve- to fourteen-hour days and Saturdays.

In the fifteen minutes that he waited for Doug to return, Oliver thought it might work. He hadn't planned on staying long anyway at the party, just enough to put in an appearance. He never felt comfortable at these things. Phillipa had said he suffered from a social anxiety disorder. He had scoffed at that but wondered from time to time if she might be right. Crowds of people made him nervous. There seemed to always be so many moving parts. It was difficult to keep track of them.

He waited for Doug, curious about his solution.

CHAPTER FIVE

Annie pulled on her coat and checked her pocket for her gloves. She made sure she had everything she needed in her briefcase and snapped it shut; she planned on doing some work at home. The action thriller was so good that translating it didn't really feel like work. She flipped the lights off in her office and yawned not once but twice. It had been a long week and she was looking forward to the weekend. It was going to start with a long, hot bath when she got home.

She locked her door, and when she looked up she caught sight of Doug trotting toward her.

"Annie!" he called out.

With her purse slung over her shoulder and her briefcase in hand, she waited until Doug reached her.

"Carol has already left. She went home early to get ready for your Christmas party," Annie said.

"I'm here to see you. I'm glad I caught you before you left."

"What can I do for you?" she asked.

"I need a favor," he started, leaning against the doorframe and tapping a finger on the door.

"Sure," she said automatically. She'd known Doug and Carol since she arrived in New York. Outside of the office, they were the only friends she had in the city. If it wasn't for them, she might never leave her apartment.

"It's . . . well, it's actually Oliver who needs the favor," Doug admitted.

Annie closed her eyes. "Forget it. That will never work out. You and Carol tried, but it's just not meant to be."

"He's in a bit of a bind," Doug said.

"Is he now?" Annie asked, not caring.

"He doesn't know anyone here."

"Oh, don't start that. That's what Carol said when she tried to fix me up with him," Annie said. Oliver had some nerve looking to her for a favor.

"Look, I wouldn't ask if the situation weren't desperate, but he *needs* a date for tonight's party," Doug said.

"Tonight? He certainly waited until the last minute," Annie said.

"His date canceled at the eleventh hour," Doug explained.

She wasn't helping Oliver Chesterfield tonight or any other night. One meeting had been enough. Although . . .

Did she want to go to Gilbert, Hardcastle, and Jones's Christmas party? Their parties were legendary. It was guaranteed to be a good time and good food, and Doug and Carol would be there, too. But it would mean she'd have to spend time in Oliver's company. At least she didn't have to worry about getting nervous—since the disaster of the blind date, he held no attraction for her.

"Maybe he could return the favor," Doug said.

"I don't need anything from him," Annie said. But as the words were floating out of her mouth, a thought occurred to her. How desperate was he? She bit her lip as her mind raced.

"All right, never mind," Doug said.

"Wait a minute, Doug," Annie said with a sigh. It went against her better judgment, but maybe an arrangement could be made.

"Aw, thanks, Annie, you're the best! So you'll do it?" Doug asked, unable to hide his disbelief.

"Maybe. I might need a favor of my own," she said.

"I think you might find him agreeable," Doug said.

Although Annie remained skeptical, she followed Doug to the bank of elevators.

As they rode the elevator up to Oliver's office, Doug explained the situation and Annie's mind raced with possibilities. Was Oliver as desperate for a date tonight as she was for a date for Rachel's wedding? She was practically holding her breath. He'd certainly look the part. If they could only get past their mutual dislike of each other, it just might work.

She saw him first. As she and Doug walked down the corridor to Oliver's office, she observed him through the glass wall of his office with his head down, leafing through paperwork on his desk. Then he looked up and spotted them.

Annie did not miss the look of surprise on Oliver's face when he spied her through the glass wall of his office. Her mood began to deteriorate and she began to sour on the idea. All she had to do was turn on her heel and head home to her bathtub.

When she entered the office, Oliver stood up.

"Annie, it's good to see you again. Please make yourself comfortable," he said, gesturing to the leather chairs in front of his desk.

"I'll leave you two to sort out the details," Doug said, and he was gone, leaving Annie alone with Oliver.

As she settled into her chair and crossed her legs, she reminded herself not to let their previous encounter color her judgment, but it was just about impossible. They had gotten off on the wrong foot. But she'd given this a lot of thought on the ride up in the elevator.

Depending on how desperate he was, she could use this to her advantage. *Would* use this to her advantage.

Once they were both seated, Oliver started. "I'm sure Doug told you about the predicament I find myself in this evening."

"He did," Annie agreed. "You need someone to pose as your girlfriend for tonight's Christmas party."

"Yes," he said, smiling. He appeared friendly, but Annie remained cautious.

She thought he should smile more; it made his personality seem less severe. He could almost pass for *dashing*, with that handsome face and enviable dark hair in a shade of auburn some women could only achieve with the help of their hairdresser. And the bonus was that accent. Every time he spoke, an image of afternoon tea with crustless sandwiches and scones with clotted cream and strawberry jam came to mind. It was a shame about his personality.

He bent his head and finally said, "I would be grateful if you could help me out."

A little humility never hurt anyone, Annie thought.

"I'd be willing to help you," she started. His shoulders lifted and she continued, "But I need a favor myself."

Oliver tilted his head to one side. "You need a favor?"

"Yes, I do. You know, like a quid pro quo," she said.

"I'm familiar with the term," he said evenly.

And although she knew what she was asking was downright crazy, she had nothing to lose. Even if he did say no, she knew she'd still go to his Christmas party with him. Not for him but because of the food the Hardcastle law firm was noted for. That alone would be worth putting up with him for the evening.

With some hesitation, Oliver asked, "What do you need?"

"My sister is getting married on Christmas Eve and I need a date for the wedding," she said, realizing with a sinking heart that he was probably going home for Christmas.

"Why?" he asked, tapping his fountain pen on the desk.

"Why what?" she asked.

"Why do you need a date for your sister's wedding?" he asked. He raised one eyebrow. "Why is it so important?"

Did she tell him? Did she divulge that much about herself to *him?*

"You already know about my predicament. If you need this favor from me, don't you think it's fair to tell me about yours?" he leveraged.

She might as well be honest with him. "My sister is engaged to a man whose brother is my ex-boyfriend," she said.

Oliver had given a nod at each part of her sentence: sister, man, brother. It was as if he was trying to keep all the players straight. She sympathized; she sometimes had a hard time juggling all the main players as well.

"I see," he said, appearing thoughtful. "You want to make your ex jealous? Prove to him that you have moved on? That you're no longer in love with him?"

She blushed at his last question. "Yes, exactly," she said, shifting uncomfortably in her chair.

"And have you moved on?" he asked.

"Of course I have," she said, indignant. Although she wasn't sure. Only time would tell.

"And what exactly do I have to do?" he asked.

"Just pretend to be my boyfriend. Now, I should tell you, my hometown is located in the middle of the state, but it could be a twenty-four-hour turnaround," she explained. "You could fly in the morning of the wedding. There's a hotel in town you could stay at. You'll be back in the city on Christmas morning so you won't have to alter your holiday plans." Even as she said this, she realized how outrageous it sounded.

"Wouldn't your family expect you to spend Christmas with your boyfriend?" he asked.

Annie hadn't thought of that. Hurriedly, she said, "We'll just say you're going home to England for Christmas."

Oliver nodded and asked, "Wouldn't they expect you to go to England with me?"

Annie shook her head. "No, of course not. I'll say I can't get off from work and that our relationship is still new."

They stared at each other, and the only sound came from the pen that Oliver continued to tap against the top of his desk.

"Are you not going home for Christmas?" she asked.

He shook his head. "Going home next week. It's the only time my brothers and I could get off work together."

Annie tried to picture more variations of him, wondering if they were older or younger and how much were they alike. She was encouraged by the fact that he had not said no outright. Unless of course he was stringing her along.

"To be clear," he said, "I'm asking you to accompany me to a Christmas party for approximately two hours, and in return you want me to take you to your sister's wedding—out of town—with a twenty-four-hour commitment." He leaned back in his chair, the fountain pen between his hands. With a smirk, he added, "It's hardly equitable."

Annie stilled her breathing. She wouldn't let him bait her. He appeared to have forgotten their previous encounter. He'd insulted her the first time and here she was, willing to help him out at the last minute.

In the end, Annie decided to call his bluff. "You're right, Oliver. It isn't equitable. I was appealing to your sense of decency."

He flinched.

Abruptly, she stood up from her chair. This idea of hers had been stupid. How could she expect him to go along with her harebrained scheme? She couldn't. Her face felt hot. "Good luck."

He scrambled to a standing position. "Wait a minute."

Annie glanced at her watch. "Look, I won't keep you a moment longer. Because you've got less than three hours to find someone to take to your Christmas party."

He blanched.

Oliver put his hands on his hips and said, "Annie Beasley, you drive a hard bargain."

CHAPTER SIX

Annie's apartment was located on the second floor of a redbrick building in Brooklyn. As soon as Oliver knocked on the door, she opened it just wide enough to slip through, and closed it behind her. He was unable to get a glimpse inside, and he wondered what she was hiding. He also wondered if she lived alone. Maybe her place was a mess. He frowned as an image of an unmade bed and a sink full of dishes appeared in his mind. He reminded himself that this was just a date; it wasn't like he was moving in with her or anything.

Her blonde hair was piled into an updo. She wore bright red lipstick that made her eyes seem bluer, reminding him of the bluebells that grew wild in the spring in the meadows back home. She really was quite pretty. It was a pity about the non-stop chatting and giggling. When he first laid eyes on her at Doug and

Carol's house, his immediate reaction had been, *This could work*. He'd found himself interested. But then the whole thing had gone downhill.

"I'm all set," she said.

He nodded. "The car's downstairs." He realized how stupid that sounded. Where would the car be? On the stairwell? In the basement of her apartment building? She had him tongue-tied. Why was that? Oliver glanced at her, all bundled up in a heavy black velvet wrap, and wondered what she was wearing beneath it, hoping at the same time it was appropriate. Maybe this hadn't been a good idea; he should have just made his excuses and not gone to the party, said he was sick or something, or just taken a chance and gone alone.

When they emerged from her building, the driver of the hired car stepped out and opened the back door for them. There was no snow but the night was crisp and cold. The moon shone brightly in an inky-black sky. From the hired car came the sounds of hip-hop Christmas music.

"Thank you," Annie said, taking Oliver's offered hand and climbing into the backseat.

Oliver followed her and settled himself into the seat next to her. He caught a glimpse of her in profile—her peaches-and-cream complexion, her strong aquiline nose, the soft curve to her lips. Her perfume was light. It had been awhile since he'd been on a date. Although this was not a real date, he reminded himself. It was strictly a mutually agreed-upon arrangement.

Oliver cleared his throat and tugged at his tie. It felt hot in the backseat of the car. He braced himself for an onslaught of chatting and nervous laughter.

Spying the bar, he asked, "Would you like a beverage?"

Annie turned her head toward him and gave him a small smile. "No, thank you."

He felt at a loss for words and it put him at a disadvantage. "Maybe we should go over a few things."

"Like what?" Annie tilted her head slightly and a curl escaped from her updo, coming to rest against her neck. It was distracting. He turned away to gather his thoughts, trying not to think about taking that curl and wrapping it around his finger.

"Maybe some background in case anyone should ask how long we've been going out, so our stories are straight," he said, not feeling comfortable with the level of deception involved.

"Okay." She nodded. "How long have we been going out?"

The first question and he was already stumped.

Annie was talking. "It should be long enough that it might be serious but not long enough that it *should* be serious."

Oliver raised his eyebrows as he considered this. It was almost a paradox. But he conceded that for tonight's purposes, she was probably right.

"Maybe two months? Three months?" she asked.

"That sounds about right," he said.

They went quiet as they both realized that that took them right back to their first meeting and their first impression of each other, which had been disastrous.

Bravely, he suggested, "Maybe we could use the actual day we met as our beginning."

"Such as it was," she said, but relented and added, "It would keep things straight."

"Maybe we could put a positive spin on it," he said.

"Good luck with that," she said tightly. She turned her head to look out the window.

An awkward silence fell between them. He hoped she wouldn't be surly during the evening. That would not bode well and might do more harm than good. He wondered if he should inquire about this but decided against it, choosing to give her the benefit of the doubt. After all, at one point Doug and Carol had tried to fix them up. And they wouldn't have fixed him up with just anybody. Or at least he hoped not.

Nothing more was said until the driver pulled up in front of the hotel in Manhattan where the Christmas party was being held. Without waiting for the car to come to a full stop, Oliver jumped out of the backseat, anxious to get some fresh air. He held open the door for Annie, extending his hand to help her out of the car.

She shivered and pulled her wrap closer to her, holding on to her clutch purse. "Thank you," she said, but she didn't look at him.

Oliver headed up the steps, hoping the evening would be a success. Since there was no romantic element to their arrangement, he convinced himself to relax. They each had a part to play. Nothing more. It was almost a relief. Looking around, he realized Annie wasn't with him. Glancing over his shoulder, he spotted her still standing at the curb with her eyebrows raised. He walked back down to her, wondering if she was having second thoughts.

"What's wrong?" he asked.

She gave him a gentle smile. "We're supposed to be a couple."

Oliver looked around and muttered, "Oh, right." He offered Annie his arm and she slipped her hand through the crook of it, and they walked together up the steps and into the hotel lobby. He had to slow his stride so Annie could keep up.

Oliver glanced down at her footwear, a pair of stilettos, and muttered, "I don't know how you women walk in those things."

Annie laughed. "It's not easy, but they look good."

He looked back down at her feet and agreed. "They do, indeed."

Once inside, they were directed to the coat check. Oliver helped Annie out of her shrug and his breath hitched in his throat. Her sapphire-blue velvet V-neck dress hugged her curves. He stood there, holding her coat over his arm, staring.

"Is it all right?" she asked, biting her lip. "Is it appropriate?"

"You look—"

"Hey, you guys made it!" Oliver and Annie turned toward the voice. Doug and Carol approached them.

"Oh, wow, Annie, your dress is gorgeous!" Carol said.

"Thank you," Annie said. She and Carol engaged in conversation as Oliver handed the coat-check attendant their coats. He tucked the receipt into his breast pocket.

"I see you managed to come to some sort of agreement," Doug said as the four of them walked through the lobby toward the ballroom.

"We did," Oliver said. Now was not the time to go into all the details and his own part in their arrangement. He wasn't sure what he had signed up for. Looking back over it, he realized she had practically swindled him. But as long as Mr. Hardcastle ended up convinced that they were a couple, then he'd soldier through twenty-four hours with her at her sister's wedding. There was no sense in griping about it. He'd made a promise and he had a duty to discharge his obligation.

"Doug and I are still hopeful for the two of you," Carol said over her shoulder.

Beside him, Annie's step faltered and Oliver reached out to steady her. Annie's smile looked as forced as his felt. Neither said a word, but Annie did slip her arm through his when he offered it.

Tables bearing huge arrangements of poinsettias and white roses were placed throughout the spacious lobby with its high ceiling. A Christmas tree took up one corner of the room, decorated all in multicolored lights and ornaments. Orchestral holiday music played subtly in the background. It was hard not to feel festive when one was wading knee-deep through holiday cheer.

Outside the main ballroom, a cream-colored placard stood on a gold easel. The placard simply read, "Gilbert, Hardcastle, and Jones."

The firm employed over one hundred people, and it appeared that everyone was there. The four of them found seats together at a table, then moved through the room to mingle. Doug and Carol went off to talk to another of Doug's colleagues.

Oliver put his hands in his pockets and rocked on his feet. Annie's eyes bounced around the room and finally settled on him. She smiled.

Oliver squinted and said, "You've got some lipstick on your teeth."

Looking down, Annie pulled a tissue out of her clutch and furiously rubbed her front teeth. She looked up at him again. "Is it gone?"

He nodded. "You have . . . nice teeth."

"Thanks."

Both looked awkwardly around.

"Look, we're going to have to get over our discomfort if we want to pull this off," Annie pointed out.

Oliver nodded. She looked smashing in that dress. How hard could it be to pretend she was his girlfriend? He decided not hard at all.

"Absolutely," he answered.

She stepped a bit closer to him. In return, Oliver inched closer to her. He sighed. He wasn't any good at small talk. He was better suited to briefs, or one-on-one conversations with people he knew well.

A server approached them with a tray of champagne. Oliver looked at Annie and she nodded. He held up his fingers to signal two, and handed one to Annie.

"Happy Christmas," he said, clinking his glass against hers.

They'd only taken one sip when another waiter approached them with various plates of appetizers. Annie frowned at the offerings.

"That's salmon mousse, liver pâté, and caviar," the server said, pointing to each one in turn.

"Caviar? I've never had caviar," Annie said.

"Then you should definitely try it," Oliver said encouragingly. He took two servings from the tray before Annie could change her mind and handed one to her.

"I will," she said, accepting the small square of toast with a bit of caviar on it. As she nibbled at it, she nodded her head, chewed thoughtfully, and her eyes grew large.

"That's yummy," she enthused. "I thought it would be gross, but it's actually quite good."

"It is, isn't it?" Oliver said. "Would you like another one?"

"Oh, yes, please," she said.

Oliver procured a few more of the appetizers and watched with interest as Annie devoured them. Her enthusiasm almost made him laugh.

Dinner was impressive: four courses that included filet mignon and lobster. After, Oliver and Annie stood up from the table as the band started playing.

"Oliver, there you are!" said a voice behind them.

They turned around to face a distinguished-looking older gentleman dressed in a suit, vest, and bow tie. An old-fashioned watch chain extended from a button to the pocket of his vest. Oliver immediately broke into a smile and extended his hand. "Mr. Hardcastle, it's good to see you."

"And you," Mr. Hardcastle said. Turning to Annie, he asked, "And who is this?"

"Mr. Hardcastle, may I introduce—uh—my girlfriend, Annie Beasley," Oliver managed to get out, his voice practically cracking.

Mr. Hardcastle looked from Annie to Oliver and then back to Annie. "If I were about fifty years younger, I'd give you a run for your money for this lady's hand."

Annie blushed and laughed.

"And what is it that you do, Annie? May I call you Annie?" he asked, leaning toward her as he spoke.

"Of course," she answered. "I work as a translator for the firm Mason & Hodges, down on the nineteenth floor."

"Very good," he said. "I've heard good things about them. What language do you translate?"

"German," she said.

Mr. Hardcastle looked impressed. "Well done, young lady."

Annie blushed, which Oliver found intriguing. He, too, was impressed by the fact that she was a translator. It sounded interesting and he reminded himself to ask her more about it.

"What do you think about our little party? Are you enjoying yourself?"

Annie nodded enthusiastically. "I've heard wonderful things about your firm's Christmas party, so I was delighted when Oliver asked me to accompany him. And as a bonus, I've discovered the joys of caviar."

Mr. Hardcastle laughed and nodded in approval. "Oliver, I've got a lot of plans for you," he said. "After the holidays, we must have a serious talk about your future with the firm."

"I'd like that very much, sir," Oliver said, beaming.

Mr. Hardcastle turned back to Annie and asked, "Young lady, is this a long-term relationship?"

Annie's face reddened to match Oliver's, and she looked at Oliver for direction but he froze. She stammered, "I hope so."

"Well, I hope so, too," Mr. Hardcastle said with a nod toward Oliver.

Oliver wanted to army-crawl out of the room.

"I must comment on your pocket watch," Annie said, deftly changing the subject. "You don't see them often enough anymore."

"It's nice to see someone from your generation knowing about them." Mr. Hardcastle smiled.

"My father is a clockmaker—was, he's retired now," Annie said.

"A clockmaker?" Mr. Hardcastle repeated. "Now that is fascinating." The elderly man pulled the watch from his vest pocket and opened it to show Annie. "This was my grandfather's. It's over a hundred years old, but it hasn't worked in years."

Oliver and Annie leaned in to inspect it. The case was engraved with detailed scrollwork. On the inside, the time had frozen at two twenty-three. Oliver wondered what Mr. Hardcastle had been doing when it stopped.

"That's beautiful," Annie said.

"It's a shame that it doesn't work," Mr. Hardcastle said. He brightened. "Would your father be willing to take a look at it? I'd be willing to pay him."

"Oh no, no," Annie protested. When Mr. Hardcastle appeared crestfallen, she hurriedly added, "No, I mean, my father wouldn't accept any money, because he loves to tinker with old clocks and watches, but nothing would make him happier than to try to fix it."

"That's wonderful," Oliver's boss said. He detached the chain from his vest and handed the watch to Annie.

Oliver didn't know if this was a good idea. He didn't really know Annie. Or her father. They might never see her or the pocket watch again.

Annie slipped the timepiece into her clutch.

Mr. Hardcastle interrupted Oliver's anxious thoughts. "She's charming, Oliver."

Oliver could only smile. But inside, he was full of turmoil. It was looking like he was in line for some kind of promotion, but at some point, he was going to have to concoct a story about breaking up with Annie.

Would that be the end of his promotion? Could she be depended on? He glanced at her. There was nothing to be done about it now. He decided not to let his anxiety over his future ruin his evening.

Once Mr. Hardcastle left them, Oliver's posture relaxed. That was done. It would be perfectly acceptable for them to depart now. He'd achieved what he wanted: made contact with Mr. Hardcastle and given him what he hoped was the right impression. Annie had been a hit. Not one to take any chances, though, he'd stay on her to get that pocket watch returned.

"That went well," Annie said.

"It did, thank you," Oliver said.

"How long do you think we need to stay?" she asked him.

"Maybe another hour?" he floated.

Annie nodded and sipped her champagne. "That's fine. We can stay longer if you like."

She leveled her gaze on him and Oliver lost his train of thought. He'd never seen a pair of eyes as translucent a shade of blue as hers. They were almost ethereal.

"Why don't we see how the evening unfolds?" he suggested.

Annie grinned.

Oliver frowned. "What's so funny?"

"Your expressions are so . . . formal," she said.

He didn't know whether to be insulted or to apologize.

Annie laid her hand on his arm and lowered her voice. "I wasn't being judgmental. I'm sorry if I sounded rude."

Oliver nodded, glancing down at her hand on his arm, which she pulled away. She had delicate hands and fingers.

"Why don't you tell me about yourself?" Annie said.

"What do you want to know?"

Annie shrugged. "Anything. How about what you like to do when you're not working?"

Oliver had to think for a minute. He'd spent so much time working that there hadn't been a lot of free time. "I like to be outside any chance I get. Walking, hiking, running." His statements reminded him of Jem, the yellow lab back home. "Do you run?"

Annie shook her head. "No, but I've got the walking down pat."

Oliver grinned. She was cheeky.

"What do you do when you go home? And where did you say that was, again?" she asked.

"I'm from Somerset, a county in the southwest of England," he answered.

"Is it nice?" she asked.

"It is," he said quietly. For a brief moment, he wondered how it would look through her eyes. Would she love it as he did? Pulling himself together, he pushed those thoughts to the outer recesses of his mind, reminding himself again that this was strictly a business arrangement and any thoughts of showing her his home were out of the question. Those kinds of thoughts were dangerous.

But still, he found himself asking, "Have you ever been to England?"

"No, but I have been to Germany," she said.

"Did you like it?" he asked.

She nodded and gushed, "I loved it. After I graduated from college, I spent a year there immersing myself in the language and culture."

"Why German? And not some other language?" he asked, surprised.

"Do you want the long version or the shortened one?" she asked with a smile.

"Long version," he said, interested in her story.

"When I went to high school, I was going to take French as a second language, but there was a mix-up, it was closed out, and I was shuffled to German. I was so angry. I had all these plans. I wanted to go to Paris after college, maybe even live there," Annie said.

Oliver nodded to encourage her to continue.

"But as it turned out, I had a natural ability for the German language and I fell in love with it," Annie said.

Oliver was mesmerized by the way her face lit up when she spoke of it.

She continued, "My teacher kept encouraging me to pursue a career in it. I did a double major in college in English and German, and by senior year I had decided to work toward a job as a translator. The best way to proceed was to immerse myself in the German culture. I lived with a host family, got a job, and it was an amazing experience."

"It sounds like it was."

"I warn you . . ." She grinned. "I make a mean Dresdner Stollen."

Oliver was familiar with the German fruit bread. "I'd love to try that sometime." That thought came out before he realized the weight of his statement. *This is not a date!* he reminded himself. Swiftly, he changed the subject. "And yet you've only been in this job in New York for the last year. Where did you work before that?"

Annie shrugged. "On my return from Germany, I met Brad, but there are no jobs for translators in my hometown."

"He wouldn't have moved somewhere else for you? New York? Somewhere you could find the sort of work you wanted?" Oliver asked.

Annie shook her head. "He couldn't. He worked for his family business back home."

Oliver nodded. "What did you do then?"

"My teacher in high school was retiring, and she reached out to me to see if I'd be interested in teaching high-school German."

"But you did make it to the city last year," Oliver said.

"Apart from my year abroad, it's the first time I've lived away from my hometown."

"Must have been a big change for you," he remarked.

"It was and I'm adjusting," she said. "I love my job." She paused, took a sip of her champagne, and said, "But it must have been an adjustment for you to move to New York."

"A little bit," he allowed. He wasn't going to tell her that he was used to traveling and living abroad while his father was in the diplomatic service. As a child, he'd spent two years in Italy. And once his father retired to England, they spent Christmases skiing in Switzerland and summers in the south of France.

A silence settled between them. Annie stared at the floor and Oliver looked around the room. The band had begun to play, and Oliver glanced in the direction of the parquet dance floor.

"Would you care to dance?" he asked.

Annie winced. "I'm not a very good dancer."

He shrugged. "So what?"

A broad smile lit up Annie's face. "Then I'd love to."

Before he could put too much thought into it, Oliver took Annie by the hand and led her to the dance floor.

Her hand was small and soft in his, and he was careful not to squeeze it too tight. He found them a space, then took Annie in his arms and whirled her around in time with the music. Annie's eyes widened and she grinned. "Wow, Oliver, you're really good at this!"

"I learned in primary school." He spun her away from him and then pulled her back.

"Really? We never had that in gym class," Annie said over the music.

"It was social dancing," Oliver explained. "Waltzes, set dancing, even some jitterbugging."

"That must have been fun," Annie said. "I would have loved to learn that."

"As a teenage boy, it was not at the top of my list but now as an adult, it's a skill that has come in handy," he admitted.

"I'll say!" Annie's cheeks were flushed with exertion and she did her best to keep up with him. Toward the end of the first round of dances, when their faces were damp and they were nearly breathless, Oliver dipped Annie until her back was practically horizontal with the floor.

"Oh!" she gasped.

Oliver looked into her eyes, thinking that the evening had turned out so much better than he had anticipated. For a moment, they held that position, eyes locked. The song came to an end and Oliver abruptly pulled Annie back up to her feet and let go of her. Neither looked at the other. Instead, they joined the rest of the crowd and clapped for the band.

Finally, Annie said, "Well that was fun."

Chapter Seven

It had been a week since Oliver's Christmas party. Other than a short text the following day, Annie had not heard from him. The text had been to the point: thanking her for her help at his Christmas party and letting her know he was looking forward to the wedding.

His party had gone a lot better than even she had anticipated. They'd spent the evening eating and drinking and dancing. The dancing! If it had been anyone else but Oliver, she would have labeled it a great date. By the time they'd left around midnight, she was almost convinced herself that they were a couple.

As soon as Annie finished work on Friday evening, she packed up her car and headed home to Hope Springs. It was late by the time she arrived, and she was surprised to see lights on in the house. Her parents must still be up. She still had a key to the house—her father had insisted on it—and had planned on going right up to bed when she arrived. As she slipped in through the front door, the grandfather clock on the upstairs landing gonged eleven. Annie set her carry-on down, pulled off her gloves, and tucked them into her coat pocket.

Her mother pushed through the kitchen door and threw up her arms. "Annie, you're here! Your father and I were waiting up for you."

Annie felt guilty. "Oh, Mom, you didn't have to wait up."

"Come on, we're back in the kitchen," her mother said.

Annie left her bag in the front hall, draped her coat over the newel post, and followed her mother back through to the kitchen. As soon as they pushed through the door, a blast of heat greeted her. The great Aga was lit and her father was shoveling wood into it as she walked in. They had affectionately named the big red range "Aggie" years ago when she and Rachel were little girls.

Her father straightened up and shut the range door. "There she is. We were starting to get worried about you."

Annie went over to him and hugged him. "I'm sorry, Dad. I was late leaving work. But the drive up was uneventful, thank goodness."

Her mother made tea and set down three mugs on the old farmhouse table, which had certainly seen its share of meals and family gatherings. It had been there for as long as Annie could remember. Her mother brought over a bowl of sugar and a pitcher of milk. She set down a pan of homemade baked squares.

"Mint bars!" Annie said. They were a chocolate-mint concoction her mother had been making since Annie was a young girl. They always reminded her of Christmas, as it was the only time of year her mother made them.

Annie fixed her tea with a little bit of sugar and milk and helped herself to a square.

"I love these," she said, biting into it. "So tell me, what needs to be done this weekend?"

"Rachel wants to get the favors done, and we need to chase down some errant invitations," her mother said.

Annie nodded, taking a sip of her tea.

"And Violet is here. She wants to help with the wedding," Peggy said, referring to Annie's young cousin, who had just turned thirteen.

"Oh good," Annie said.

"She fell asleep on the couch and we sent her up to bed," Malcolm said.

Annie cradled her mug in her hands, looking around the kitchen, thinking it was wonderful to be home. She looked up to see both her parents staring at her, their cups of tea sitting in front of them, untouched.

Annie looked from her mother to her father. "What? What's wrong?"

Peggy shrugged and looked at her husband, who raised an eyebrow in return.

"What's going on?" Annie asked. "Is everything all right? You don't seem upset, but somehow you seem like you're holding something back."

Her mother finally picked up her cup of tea and peered over the rim of it. "Now who's calling the pot black? I think you've been bag sanding us all this time."

"I'm not sandbagging you," Annie said, taking another bite of her mint bar. If she didn't have to fit into that bridesmaid gown, she'd help herself to another bar. In her experience, bridesmaid dresses tended to run small in size.

Her father leaned forward on the table, a smile on his face. "Your mother and I were just wondering about your gentleman friend. You mentioned to her last month that you were bringing him to the wedding but haven't said a word about it since." His expression softened and he added, "And we didn't want to pry."

Which was exactly what they were doing.

"Oh—Oliver!" Annie said.

Her mother threw her head back and laughed, then mimicked Annie. "'Oh—Oliver!' Really, Annie!" She paused and said, "We know nothing. We'd like to know something. Anything. Come on, throw us a scrap."

Both her parents stared at her. Did they view her as someone who was desperate? The first sign of a man in her life and they were breathing a big sigh of relief?

"Well, his name is Oliver Chesterfield and he's an attorney at Gilbert, Hardcastle, and Jones. He works in the same building I do," Annie told them.

"Gilbert, Hardcastle, and Jones," Peggy repeated. "I like the sound of that."

"Oh, and he's British," Annie added.

"British, really?" Her mother beamed. "That's exciting!"

Was it? Annie wondered. She supposed it was.

"Is he nice?" her mother asked.

Beside her, her father sighed. "Of course he's nice. Our Annie wouldn't be going out with him if he wasn't."

"How did you meet?" her mother pressed. Annie should have known that her mother would want all the details.

"My friends Carol and Doug set us up. Oliver works with Doug. That's how we all know each other," Annie explained.

"And he's coming here for the wedding?" her father asked, thumping a finger on the table excitedly.

"Yes." Annie nodded, sipping her tea. Her eyelids were beginning to droop. "I've got to remember to book him into the hotel in town."

Peggy frowned. "Not at the hotel. He can stay here with us. With family."

Annie paled. "No, I think he'd feel more comfortable at the hotel."

"There's plenty of room here, Annie, and we would love to get to know him better," her mother said.

"He's only going to be here for twenty-four hours. He's flying back to the city early Christmas morning," Annie said.

Her mother looked horrified. "He's not spending Christmas with you?"

Annie shook her head. "Nah, it's still a new relationship, we're both okay with spending Christmas apart."

Peggy went to protest, but her husband covered her hand with his. "Annie and Oliver know what's best. Leave it be, Peggy."

Peggy bit her lip.

Annie stood up from the table and stretched. "I'm going to bed, I'm beat," she said, carrying her teacup over to the sink.

Her parents stood up.

"We'll see you in the morning for breakfast," her mother said. "We've got a lot to do this weekend for the wedding."

"Good night, Mom, good night, Dad," Annie said, slipping out the door, yawning.

"Good night," they called after her.

The smell of bacon and coffee woke Annie the following morning. Bright winter sunlight shone through the window, and she looked around her old room.

Oh, Mom.

A portion of the room was packed with paper and canned goods from the floor to the ceiling. Her mother was a coupon queen and a lover of all things buy-one-get-one-free. Annie studied the tower of paper towels and hoped it wouldn't end up falling all over the place.

Deciding to ignore it for now, she jumped out of bed. After she showered and dressed, she bounded down the stairs to the kitchen in search of food and more specifically, coffee.

At the kitchen table were Grandma Fischer, Grandpa Beasley, and her sister, Rachel. Cousin Violet sat next to Grandma Fischer. Peggy stood at the stove, and she turned to Annie, smiled, and said, "Sunny-side up?"

"Perfect, Mom, thanks," Annie said.

Rachel jumped up and hugged her. "Oh, Annie, it's so good to see you."

"So, it's to be a Christmas wedding," Annie teased her.

When they pulled apart, Grandma Fischer said, "Although why there's such a rush to get married is beyond me. You'd think there was a baby on the way or something."

"Grandma!" Rachel warned.

"Just saying, that's all," Grandma Fischer said. Their grandmother was a tiny woman who was a long-standing member of the blue-rinse brigade and smelled like blueberries from the electronic cigarette she constantly smoked.

Grandpa Beasley looked up from his cup of black coffee. "And even if there were a baby on the way, so what? That used to happen a lot more than you think." He sipped his coffee as he reflected. "My own mother used to say that the first baby comes at any time, but the second baby takes nine months."

"Wise woman," Grandma Fischer said. "Were you adopted?"

Grandpa Beasley laughed, his belly shaking. "You're as mean as a snake, Frieda."

"How have you two been?" Annie asked, inserting herself between her grandmother and grandfather, kissing each one on the forehead. Her grandmother patted Annie's arm and her grandfather took hold of her other hand and kissed it on the palm.

"I check the obituaries every morning to see if I died," Grandma Fischer said, "but I'm still here. I think the good Lord forgot me." Grandma was well into her eighties, and Grandpa wasn't far behind her.

"Are you sure he forgot about you?" Grandpa Beasley asked, grinning. "Don't you think it's presumptuous to assume you're going to heaven?" Under his breath, he muttered, "More like H, E, double hockey sticks."

Annie laughed and elbowed him.

"Hello, Violet," Annie said.

Violet stood and let Annie wrap her in a warm embrace. The young girl smelled of pancake syrup and cinnamon. Violet was the only child of Uncle Al and Aunt Betty. She'd been a total surprise. After years of infertility, Aunt Betty had her at forty-two. As she was the youngest of Grandma Fischer's three granddaughters, she'd been spoiled since the day she was born.

"I hear you're going to help with the wedding."

"I am," the girl said, enthused. Annie tucked one stray lock of hair behind Violet's ear.

"That's great, because we need all the help we can get," Annie said.

The young girl nodded enthusiastically, her ponytail bobbing behind her. Annie noticed her white T-shirt. It depicted a heart-shaped Union Jack and in cursive, it said, "Royally obsessed."

"I love your shirt," Annie said.

Violet loved anything to do with the royal family, especially the weddings. For the most recent one, she'd slept over and got up with Annie, Rachel, and Peggy at five-thirty in the morning to watch it on the television. Her love of all things royal was fervent, and her parents had already taken her on two trips to England.

Peggy set a plate of bacon and eggs in front of Annie.

"Thanks, Mom." Annie turned to her grandmother and said, "Maybe your work here isn't done yet."

Grandma Fischer scowled. "I don't care whether it is or it isn't. I'm ready to go. I've already got my funeral outfit picked out."

"Oh, Mom, don't talk like that," Peggy said. "You wouldn't want to miss the wedding."

Grandma shrugged, taking a drag on her electronic cigarette.

"Besides, Grandma, don't you want to meet Annie's new boyfriend?" Violet asked, grinning. She leaned forward, her young eyes alight. "He's British!"

Grandma peered at Annie. "It's a new boyfriend, is it?"

Annie laughed. "Yes, Grandma."

Her grandmother smiled. A smile from Grandma Fischer was as rare as a sighting of Halley's comet, so Annie took this as a good sign.

"That Brad wasn't good enough for you," Grandma said.

Grandpa Beasley pushed his plate away, pulled out a cigar, and chomped on it, unlit. "On this one point, I have to agree with Frieda. He wasn't for you, Annie, my dear."

"Thanks, Grandma and Grandpa," Annie said.

"Just speaking the truth," Grandma said.

"Um, hello, I'm marrying his brother," Rachel said from across the table.

"We know that, dear, but he isn't Brad," Grandma pointed out. "Thank goodness."

"No, Brian's all right," Grandpa concluded.

Rachel looked at them in confusion, but Grandma focused her attention on Annie. "I understand your young man will be joining us for the wedding."

"He will," Annie replied.

"Mom, are you almost finished?" Peggy asked. "You've got an appointment to get your hair done."

Annie was grateful for the change in conversation if only to discourage any further discourse on Oliver. She had spared a thought about him from time to time. They came unbidden, and that worried her. He'd been such a gentleman at the party. One didn't have to be a rocket scientist to know that he had been brought up well. There was probably a bit of money there behind him. And him coming to her sister's wedding now made her nervous. How would he fit in? Would he fit in? Or would he feel as if he'd just parachuted into the Island of Misfit Toys?

His firm's Christmas party had been one thing. A public affair for employees with the founding member of the firm present had everyone on their best behavior. Oliver's singular objective had been pulled off beautifully.

But her family was no high-end law firm, and her objective wasn't a promotion. Her family was nuts—but in a good way—and she wondered about him fitting in. Not that her family wouldn't love him; she just wasn't so sure if Oliver would love them. Also, her objective was twofold: to prove to Brad that not only had she gotten over him but she had moved on. And Oliver presented the right image of getting on with one's life.

Regularly, she reminded herself that it was only twenty-four hours. Oliver would be back home in time for Christmas. Hopefully, unscathed. All these things ran through her head as she bit into her toast.

After breakfast, Annie found her father in his study, otherwise known as the clock room. As a child, she'd loved this room. Every surface, from walls to corners to tabletops, was covered in various types of clocks. A non-working grandmother clock stood in one corner. A cuckoo clock opened on the hour, every hour, the little bird popping out to announce the time with his cuckoo calls. When she and Rachel were little, they'd sit on the armchair, fascinated, patiently waiting for the bird to emerge. There was only one spot on the wall where a painting hung, and it was a replica of Franz Krischke's *Still Life with Clock* in a heavy, ornate gold frame. Despite the chaos of the room, there was comfort in the symphony of ticking.

Her father was behind his workbench, seated on a high stool. An architect lamp on the desk illuminated his work space, where all his tools were laid out before him. An old library card catalog, behind him, held the guts of countless watches and clocks he'd worked on over the years, little bits and bobs whose purpose were a mystery to Annie, but her father knew every little piece in this room and what it was for. He looked up when Annie entered the room.

"Hello, Annie," he said. "Sit down."

Annie did that, pulling up the second stool and occupying the space across the table from her father. She laid Mr. Hardcastle's watch on the table.

Her father looked up at her and said, "What do we have here?"

"It belongs to Oliver's boss, but it doesn't work anymore. He was hoping you might be able to fix it."

Her father looked pleased and picked up the watch to examine it further. "I would love to try."

Annie smiled. Her father always said that, and then he always fixed them. No matter how long it took.

Her father read the face of the watch. "American Waltham Watch Company. They've been around a long time."

"Have they?" she asked, settling in.

Her father removed the back of the watch and studied the mechanics. "Hmm. I see."

Annie stayed silent, leaving her father to concentrate.

She laid her elbow on the table, rested her head in her hand, and watched her father work.

"You know, I'm glad to hear that you've got a boyfriend," he said, not looking up from his work.

"Me, too." She smiled weakly.

"I've been worried about you."

"You have? Why?" she asked. The thought of her father worrying about her upset her. She didn't want that.

He casually shrugged, leaning forward, the light of the lamp casting his face in the spotlight. When had his hair gone so gray? But yet his eyes were still an amazing blue.

Without breaking his concentration, he began to take the pieces out of the back of the watch's mechanism. "After your breakup, you left for New York in a hurry. And although I understand the motive behind it, I wonder if you're as happy as you're telling us you are," he said quietly. He looked up at her and searched her face.

"I'm fine, Dad," she said, her voice cracking. She coughed quickly to cover it up. "Why would you think I wasn't?"

Her father returned his attention to the watch. "At times, when you're telling us about your life in New York, it just seems that you're trying to convince yourself, as well, that it's wonderful."

"It is wonderful," she said, trying to muster up some enthusiasm. "I love my job. It's like a dream come true." Which it was.

Her father nodded. "That's great, but you need to have balance. It can't be all about work."

"Or clocks." She grinned.

"Touché," he said with a laugh.

Her father set the watch down and sat up straight on his stool.

"But seriously, Annie, it's okay if it doesn't work out. There's nothing to be embarrassed about," he said.

Annie felt as if he were reading her mind. "Well, no," she stammered. "I know that."

"Don't feel that if you decide to come home you've got to put your tail between your legs," he said.

"Oh, I wouldn't," she said hurriedly. Although she probably would. What would it say about her if she came back home after only a year? Hardly setting the world on fire. It would feel like a failure. "But I'm not ready to come home."

She was half sure about that.

Her father nodded and leaned forward, resuming his work. "All right then, Annie. But just know the door is always open and you can return any time."

"Thanks, Dad," she said, biting her lip. With a nod toward the watch, she asked, "Do you think you can fix it?"

"I think I can," he said with a satisfied smile and a gleam in his eye.

In the afternoon, Annie sat down with Rachel and their mother to talk about wedding favors. Violet had been appointed secretary and had a variety of colored pens laid out in front of her and a pink cloth binder, which she had decorated with stickers and glitter-covered words that read, "Rachel and Brian's Christmas Wedding." She'd alternated each letter with red and green glitter. Malcolm had retreated to the clock room after lunch to work on Mr. Hardcastle's watch, declaring it "a beauty." Grandpa Beasley and Grandma Fischer were in the living room, reading and watching television. They had worked out a system years ago as to who got to pick what to watch: they alternated days. It spared everyone a lot of grief.

"What were you thinking of doing for wedding favors?" Annie asked.

"How about gift bags of potpourri? You know, Christmas scented, like bayberry or pine cones," Peggy suggested helpfully.

Annie liked that idea and nodded in agreement. But Rachel scrunched up her nose. "No, not *that*." She scowled. With a laugh, she added, "Next, you'll suggest candy-coated almonds."

"When I was your age, candy-coated almonds were the *soup du jour* at every wedding," Peggy said with a sniff.

Annie knew what her mother meant but continued, "What did you have in mind?"

Rachel whipped out her phone, tapped and scrolled, and announced, "This. I found this on Pinterest."

Annie cringed. She loved Pinterest but everything *looked* so easy and, in the end, the craft or life hack ended up looking like a third-grader did it. Annie, her mother, and Violet leaned over Rachel's phone when she passed it to them.

The photo depicted a row of mason jars filled with hot cocoa mix and topped off with marshmallows. Around the rim of each jar was a candy cane with a green ribbon.

"Oh, that's cute," Peggy declared.

Violet smiled. "Everyone loves hot cocoa, especially at Christmas."

They all nodded in agreement.

"But where are we going to get all that cocoa mix and mason jars?" Dollar signs floated in front of Annie's eyes. She didn't want to have to be the one to remind them that it was a low-budget wedding.

"I've been buying bulk hot chocolate powder every payday for the last few weeks," Rachel said.

"And what about the jars?" Annie asked. She didn't treasure the thought of driving all over town in search of one hundred plus mason jars.

"There are boxes and boxes of them in the basement," Peggy said enthusiastically.

Annie frowned. "There are?"

Peggy shrugged. "Years ago, I had a brilliant venture business idea. I was going to can pears and peaches and set up a roadside stand."

"You were?" Annie asked, surprised, and wondering where she'd been when her mother was thinking of doing all this. "When was this?"

"Oh, I don't know, maybe five or ten years ago," Peggy replied.

"What happened?" Rachel asked.

"I bought the mason jars at a clearance sale in the spring, but the pear tree died and well, it didn't pan out," their mother explained.

"All right, we'll bring the jars up from the basement, run them through the dishwasher, and we can work on these tonight and tomorrow before I head back to the city," Annie said.

"Aw, thanks, Annie," Rachel said.

"That's what sisters are for."

Rachel was four years younger than Annie and when they were growing up, it seemed as if she was always tagging along or there was the instruction from their mother to "bring your sister with you." And that had led to resentment. But now, Rachel was a grown woman, working at the bank in town and about to be married, and Annie wanted to help as much as she could.

Their mother got up and brought over a platter of homemade Christmas cookies. Annie's mouth watered at the sight of the meringue kisses, snickerdoodles, and Hershey's peanut butter blossoms.

"Come on, girls, it's Christmas," their mother encouraged.

Violet immediately reached for a cookie. Annie envied her pre-adolescent self, not having to worry about her weight.

"Mom, I need to fit into my dress," Rachel moaned.

"Me, too," Annie said. Her dress was a red satin affair that clung to every bit of her. She liked it and it was certainly Christmassy. Still, she helped herself to one cookie. Rachel caved and took one for herself, too.

"Tell me about this Oliver," Rachel said.

Annie smiled and reminded herself not to elaborate too much. "He's nice. Works in the same building as me. Our friends set us up." Everything she'd said was the truth.

"Is it serious?"

Annie shrugged. "It's too early to tell."

"What about Brad?" Rachel asked, her eyebrows knitting together.

The cookie that was on the way to their mother's mouth froze midair, and she looked quickly at Annie.

"What about Brad?" Annie repeated, scowling. She was aware of Violet, nibbling a cookie, her eyes traveling back and forth between them.

"He *is* the best man, and you're the maid of honor," Rachel said.

"So?"

"I just thought it would be great if the two of you got back together," Rachel said. "And what's more romantic than getting back together at a Christmas wedding?"

"What about Oliver?" Annie asked. A small part of her felt protective and defensive about Oliver. Rachel hadn't even met him and she was already willing to chuck him out in favor of Brad. *Not so fast,* Annie thought.

Rachel munched on her cookie thoughtfully. "You and Oliver haven't been going out that long, and you and Brad have history."

Annie stared. Could her sister think that getting back together with Brad was an option? Annie glanced over at her mother, who was helping herself to another snickerdoodle. Peggy shrugged helplessly. Violet continued to eat cookies, saying nothing, her wide eyes traveling back and forth between the three of them.

Rachel must have seen the look on Annie's face, because she leaned forward, broke into a grin and said, "Wouldn't it be wonderful if you got back with Brad and I was married to Brian? We'd all be together! Our two families united! And you and I would see each other at every family gathering and holiday."

"Life is very rarely that tidy," Peggy said.

Annie didn't know where this sudden interest of Rachel's in a reconciliation between her and Brad was coming from. "Rachel, Brad left me to go traveling, remember?" Had they forgotten how heartbroken she'd been when he decided he wanted to travel the world? Alone? It was the catalyst that had sent her to New York. He knew how she'd caught the travel bug when she went to Germany, and how eager she was to explore new places.

"He's changed," Rachel said. "You'll see. He's anxious to see you."

"Why?" Annie asked. She could barely hide her disbelief.

Rachel sighed in frustration. "Because maybe he still has feelings for you."

"He missed his chance," Annie said, feeling anger beginning to overtake her. This possibility unnerved her. "I'm with Oliver now."

"But is that really going to work out?" Rachel asked. "What if Oliver decides he wants to move back to England?"

Annie felt her mother's eyes on her. Her neck felt hot. "Whatever happens between Oliver and me is between the two of us. It's nobody else's business."

"I'm sorry, I didn't mean to get you upset," Rachel said. "I was just thinking it would be nice if you and Brad got back together and you moved back to Hope Springs and we could see more of you."

Annie's anger dissipated and she sighed. "Rachel, I do miss you, but I'm just not ready to move back to Hope Springs yet. And that has nothing to do with Oliver. After Brad and I broke up, I needed a change of scenery."

Rachel nodded, but Annie wondered if she truly understood.

"Anyway, what do you say about going out for dinner tonight?" Rachel said. "I love going out to eat at Christmas because I get to see all the decorations and everyone is in a good mood."

"Oh, I don't know, there's so much to do. I've got to go back to the city tomorrow," Annie said, though she would have loved to go out for a bite to eat. She couldn't remember the last time she was in a restaurant.

"Go out for dinner," Peggy encouraged them. "If you girls bring up the boxes from the basement, I can run the jars through the dishwasher tonight and we can make the wedding favors tomorrow before Annie leaves."

Annie shrugged. "All right then." She looked at their younger cousin, Violet, and asked, "Would you like to come with us to dinner?"

"She doesn't want to hang out with us," Rachel said quickly. Annie frowned at her. She didn't want Violet's feelings to be hurt.

"I'm going to stay here with Aunt Peggy," the young girl said. "She said we're going to bake cookies and bars tonight."

"Will it just be the two of us?" Annie asked.

Rachel hesitated.

Annie narrowed her eyes. "Who else?"

"Brian . . . and Brad," Rachel replied.

Annie stood up from the table and said emphatically, "No way."

"But it will be fun!"

"For who?" Annie cried.

"The four of us: the bride, the groom, the maid of honor, and the best man," Rachel said, her tone plaintive.

Annie shook her head and said firmly, "No, Rachel, it's not going to happen."

Rachel went to protest but Peggy interrupted and said quietly, "Leave it, Rachel."

Rachel looked from her mother to Annie and back again.

Annie sighed. "Come on, let's bring those jars up from the basement."

Annie walked to work early Monday morning, thinking that she and Oliver might just be able to pull it off for the wedding. Before she'd left her parents' house, she and her mother, her sister, and her cousin had spent Sunday morning sipping Peggy's homemade eggnog and making up all one hundred and fifty wedding favors. Rachel made no more mention of Brad, and Annie was relieved. Hopefully, that was a subject put to bed once and for all. Despite the hiccough of almost getting roped into meeting up with Brad at dinner, it had been a fun weekend.

After a lunch eaten at her desk, she made her way to Oliver's office, with Mr. Hardcastle's pocket watch in her hand.

The law firm was decorated for Christmas tastefully and subtly. There were no twinkling lights hanging crookedly along the perimeter of the ceiling or a Christmas tree with plastic garland or a dearth of ornaments. Instead, an expensive-looking artificial tree stood in the corner of the reception area, lush with gold lights and Victorian-style ornaments. As hard as she tried, Annie could not see one bare spot. In the background, orchestral holiday music played softly, all the tunes recognizable. The area beneath the tree was packed with wrapped gifts. On the end table next to a reception chair, a plastic placard encouraged donations of a wrapped gift for the needy.

She approached the reception desk.

"I'm here to see Oliver Chesterfield," Annie said.

The receptionist, with a beautiful head of red hair, looked up with a smile of perfect teeth and asked, "Do you have an appointment?"

"No," she said, realizing she should have called first instead of just dropping in.

"And your name?"

"Annie Beasley."

The receptionist nodded, pressed a button, and spoke into her headset. "Mr. Chesterfield, there's an Annie

Beasley here to see you." A pause and then, "All right, thank you."

The receptionist removed her headset and stood up. "He can see you, Miss Beasley. I'll take you to his office."

"That's not necessary, I know where it is," Annie said.

The receptionist hesitated. "Are you sure?"

"I am, thank you," Annie said. She headed down the corridor before the receptionist could change her mind. All this politeness and civility were beginning to give her a headache. The atmosphere of the office was subdued. There were snippets of muted conversations, but none of the raucous laughter or raised voices you would expect from a firm of this size.

A smile appeared on Oliver's face when he spotted her. He rose from his chair. His desk was covered with files, and papers were strewn all over the place. He had dark circles under his eyes.

"Annie, come in, it's good to see you," he said, smiling. "Will you sit down?"

Glancing again at his desk, she said, "I won't, as I can see you're busy." She handed the pocket watch to him. "My father was able to fix it."

Oliver popped open the watch and smiled. "That's brilliant. I'll make sure Mr. Hardcastle gets this." He snapped the watch closed and looked at her. "Thank you, and I'll thank your father myself when I meet him."

Annie nodded. Her father had spent the whole weekend working on it, but she knew that he had enjoyed it. There was nothing he would rather be doing than tinkering with clocks and watches. Especially old ones.

"I just wanted to go over a few things with you," she said.

"Are you sure you won't sit down? Would you like some coffee or tea, perhaps?" he asked.

"No, thank you," she replied, sitting down in the nearest chair.

It was the type of office where one phone call would be placed and as if by magic, a linen-covered cart would appear with a white china teapot and matching teacups.

In less than a week, she would be parading Oliver all over Hope Springs as her boyfriend. How crazy was that? The overhead lighting of his office highlighted the streaks of red running through his beautiful mop of hair. The urge to run her hand through it gripped her. She frowned, pushing away those sorts of thoughts. This was strictly business. He'd made it clear he wasn't interested. Just because they had had a good time at his Christmas party didn't mean that she should start falling for him.

Oliver was looking at her and reflexively, she wiped whatever it was he was staring at off her face.

"What?" she asked, nervously.

"I had an interesting phone call this morning," Oliver started. He grinned like a Cheshire cat.

Annie frowned, not comprehending. But also wary.

"Your mother rang me."

"My mother?" Annie repeated, leaning forward, her eyes practically bulging out of her head. How could that have happened?

"She sounds like a lovely woman," he said.

"Why was my mother calling you?" she asked, her eyes narrowing. Mentally, she went over a list of improbable reasons her mother could have for contacting Oliver. And where had she gotten his phone number? Annie almost slapped her forehead. In casual conversation, she had told her mother Oliver's name and where he worked. Her mother might mix up words and their meanings and be a hoarder, expert level, but she was also very resourceful and when she wanted to find something out, she did.

"What did she want?" Annie asked as a curtain of impending doom began to come down.

"First, she wanted to introduce herself," he said, never taking his eyes off her.

Annie tried to control her emotions so they didn't play out across her face. Her mother was also crafty. There was no way she had called Oliver for a casual meet and greet. Nope. Her mother had had an agenda, Annie was sure of it.

"Did she, now?" Annie asked, her voice sounding much higher than she intended.

"She did."

"And . . . ?" The need to be alert for a conversation had never been more critical.

"And, she extended an invitation to stay at your home instead of the hotel for the wedding," Oliver said.

Annie sank back into her chair. No matter what happened, Oliver could not stay with them. In her home. No way. It just wouldn't work out. What would she do with him, underfoot like that for twenty-four hours? Entertain him while she played maid of honor? And what about Grandma? Oliver might not understand her grandmother's humor the way her family did. They were used to it. Annie had grown up with it. No, this couldn't happen. She needed Oliver safely ensconced at a hotel. Far away from her home. It was for his own good.

"What did you say?" she asked, holding her breath.

"I said fine. She seemed so insistent, and I thought it might be nicer than staying at a hotel," he said.

Nothing could be further from the truth. Maybe she would stay in the hotel. This was a train wreck waiting to happen.

"Are you sure?" she asked. She had to tread carefully here; she didn't want to scare him to the point where he backed out of being her date for the wedding. "Would you be comfortable staying at our home? We're a bunch of strangers."

Oliver shrugged. "It wouldn't bother me. I've got quite an extended family myself."

Not like mine, Annie thought wryly.

The conversation lagged but Oliver picked up the thread. "Your mother also asked me if I'd like to spend Christmas with your family."

Annie tried to control the tremor in her voice, tried not to betray her emotion. "Oh," finally escaped her lips.

Oliver looked steadily into her face. "I thought it might be nice to have somewhere to go for Christmas."

No. Nope. She was not going to start feeling sorry for him just because he was far away from his own home and family for Christmas or that he had nowhere to go for the holiday. That would only lead her to do something stupid, like agreeing to her mother's plan.

Annie gulped, her stomach in knots, and said, "What did you say to that?"

Oliver hesitated. "I said I'd talk it over with you."

"Oh."

"But I get the feeling you're not too keen on the idea." He didn't seem sad or anything. He appeared to be stating a fact. And he had guessed it.

"No, no, no," Annie said quickly. Now she felt like a heel. "I mean, I'll be busy and such, but you're more than welcome. Of course you're welcome to spend Christmas with us. I can't guarantee that it will be anything great." She laughed nervously, her voice taking on a higher pitch. "I mean, we've got a houseful of personalities. There's my parents, my sister, and Grandma Fischer and Grandpa Beasley who live with us." She tried to stop talking. But she couldn't. "It's nothing grand. We just hang around on Christmas Day, it's nothing special—and my parents take a nap during the afternoon, so we hardly see them at all—"

"Annie, it's all right, I don't want to make you uncomfortable," Oliver said.

"I wouldn't be uncomfortable," Annie lied.

"Why don't we compromise?" Oliver suggested.

"How?" Annie asked, doubtful.

"I'll come up to Hope Springs from the twenty-second to the twenty-sixth as your mother suggested."

"Four days, huh?" Annie asked, her heart sinking, trying not to panic.

"But I'll stay in a hotel," Oliver said.

How could she refuse him? On Christmas morning, she'd be thinking of him alone in the city with no Christmas dinner in sight. And it would ruin the holiday for her. Begrudgingly, she said, "Okay, that works. As long as you don't mind."

"Not at all. I'm looking forward to spending Christmas in a small town."

"Oh, it's small, all right," she muttered. "I better get back to work." She had to get out of there before he had any other ideas.

"I'll book my flight, and could you recommend a hotel?" he said.

"Don't worry about the hotel, I'll book that for you." Annie added it to her mental list of things to do, which was now burgeoning. She bit her lip.

"You look overwhelmed," he said.

Annie forced a bright smile. She felt that trying to pull off the charade for one day was definitely doable. But four days? Almost impossible. Hopefully, her family would be too busy with everything to notice.

"I guess we're all set then," she said. "Let me know what time your plane lands, and I'll pick you up."

"That isn't necessary, I could get a taxi," he said.

"No, I'll pick you up," she said firmly. She couldn't have the likes of him running around loose in Hope Springs.

"Are you sure?" he asked. "I don't want to put you to any extra trouble."

"It's not any trouble at all," she said truthfully. She couldn't admit to him that it would be a great deal of trouble if she didn't pick him up. There was no way he was arriving at her parents' house unannounced. Alone.

She had to manage his insertion into her family life as best she could.

"Anything else?" he asked.

"Um, not that I can think of," she said. There were a million things that worried her, but there wasn't time to go through them all.

Oliver appeared to be wrestling with something. "Is it still your goal to make this ex-boyfriend of yours jealous?" he asked, studying her face.

His gaze was intense and Annie felt the heat creep up her neck.

"Of course," she stammered. "That is, if you think we can pull it off."

Oliver leaned back. "I'll give it my personal best."

Annie didn't know whether to be reassured or scared. "Maybe we could meet up for a drink sometime before then, you know, to get to know each other better," Annie suggested, her voice cracking.

But Oliver was shaking his head. "I can't."

She stood abruptly. "No problem. I'll let you get back to work and I'll see you in Hope Springs," she said, turning to leave.

"Wait, Annie," he said with a laugh. "I mean I can't because I'm flying home on Wednesday to celebrate Christmas with my family."

"Oh, right," Annie said.

"It's going to be a quick visit," he said, "but it will be nice to see everyone."

"Of course," she said, wondering what his family was like and somehow doubting they were anything like hers. They were probably normal. Boy, was he in for a surprise when he met the Beasley clan.

Chapter Eight

It was good to be back home in England, even if it was only for a few days, to celebrate Christmas early with his family. Oliver had landed at Heathrow late the previous day and made the journey down to his parents' home in a rental car, pleased to find them looking well—tanned and fit after a stay at their vacation home in Portugal. The house would be bustling with activity with him, his two older brothers, and their families.

Oliver arrived at the breakfast table to find his parents already there, along with Sophie, the wife of his older brother James.

"Good morning, Mother," he said, bending down to kiss her on the cheek. "Am I late or early?"

"Late," she said with an indulgent smile. "I thought you'd be tired so I told Mary not to wake you."

"Thank you," he said. He helped himself to breakfast from the various dishes laid out on the sideboard.

"James and Andrew have taken the children ice skating," his mother said.

"I might join them," Oliver said.

"You should," Sophie said. "The children would love to see you. They've missed you."

Oliver pulled out a chair and sat down next to his father, removing a linen napkin from the table and laying it across his lap. "And I've missed them! I haven't seen them since last Christmas. They must have gotten so big!"

"You should be having children of your own," his mother said, voicing an oft-repeated conversation.

"Someday," he said.

"Someday? You should be looking for a nice girl to settle down with," his mother said.

"No worries, Mother, there's plenty of time. Besides, I like being the fun uncle." He grinned.

"You can't be the fun uncle forever," his mother fretted, adding after a brief pause, "I hear Phillipa is down from London."

"I know, we've been in touch," Oliver said, buttering his toast.

His mother perked up. "You have? Will you see her while you're home?"

"Oh, I don't know," he said, reaching for the bowl of orange marmalade.

"Why don't you invite her to our Christmas party?" she said easily. Oliver smiled at his mother. She was clever. She'd been angling to fix him up with Phillipa since he was in short pants.

His father peeked out from behind the newspaper. "Helen, you promised you wouldn't nag him about finding a girlfriend while he was home." He folded up the paper, laid it beside his plate, and looked at his youngest son.

"Fancy any of the American women? I hear they can be quite forthright."

Oliver laughed. It was his father's way of saying bossy. "I work with a lot of women but none that I'd be interested in."

That wasn't completely true. He'd been too busy at work to come up for air, let alone look for a girlfriend. He'd discovered he liked American women, generally. He found them confident and honest, and those were very attractive features.

"Oliver, I hate the thought of you spending Christmas alone, just hate it," his mother said.

"I'm not spending Christmas alone. I'm going to be spending it with friends," he said. He thought it was somewhat truthful. Maybe he and Annie weren't friends but since his work Christmas party, they were friendlier toward each other than they'd been.

"I'm relieved to hear that," his mother said.

Oliver nodded, not wanting to open himself up to too many questions.

"That's wonderful, son," his father said, slapping him on the back. "Christmas is a day that should be spent with family and if not family, then friends."

Internally, Oliver debated telling them about Annie. Finally, he decided he wouldn't, because his mother would be all over it. Quite possibly demanding to meet her. It wasn't necessary, as it was just a mutual arrangement. After Christmas, he'd probably never see Annie again.

"Darling, Sophie asked you a question," his mother prompted.

Oliver looked up at his sister-in-law. "I'm sorry, Sophie, what did you say?"

"How do you like New York?" she asked.

He nodded, wiping his mouth on his napkin. "I like it very much, thank you. It's an exciting place to be. It's as busy at two in the morning as it is at eight."

"Oh, that sounds dreadful." His mother grimaced as she sipped tea from her cup.

Oliver smiled at her, deciding not to remind her that she was a Londoner by birth and upbringing. When she'd married his father fifty years ago, she'd come down to Somerset and immediately fallen in love with it. She had never wanted to return to London to live.

"Well, we're glad you like it," his father said with a smile. "And remember, whatever friends you make in New York are always welcome here."

Oliver smiled. His father made it sound as if he were in his first year at primary school. But they'd always treated him like a baby—that's what he was to them. His brothers were well into their teens when he'd arrived—a pleasant surprise, his father always said about him.

"What are your plans for the day?" his father asked.

"I think after ice skating, I may head into town and meet up with some of my mates," he said. "I spoke to Peter before I left New York."

"His mother says he's still seeing that Tilly Hitchcock-Bayers, and it might be serious."

Oliver shrugged.

"I don't think Cecelia is fond of the girl," his mother said of Peter's girlfriend.

Oliver shrugged at that, too.

His mother set her teacup down on the table. "Is there no way you can come home for Christmas? It will be so lonely here without you," she said, her voice a pleading tone.

"Afraid I can't, Mother, work and all that."

"Oh, those Americans. They only take off on Christmas Day, and then everyone's back to work the day after. How do they stand that? The holidays are meant to be enjoyed."

"Leave the boy alone, Helen," his father said.

Oliver decided not to mention that most people at work were taking the week off. That would only lead to more questions. He wolfed down the rest of his breakfast and stood up. "Mother, are my skates still in the boot room?" he asked.

"They're wherever you last left them," she said, uninterested. "I'd hardly be wearing them, now would I? Ice skates are ghastly looking."

Oliver grinned but said nothing, choosing not to remind her that when he was young, she took him ice skating on the pond all the time.

Oliver traversed the countryside, cutting through the snow. His skates were slung over his shoulder. The small ionic temple with its circular dome soon came into view. His great-great-grandfather had built the edifice after his grand tour of Europe. Years ago, his father put in the pond for James, Andrew, and Oliver to enjoy.

His nieces and nephews spotted him as they skated around the frozen pond, and shouts of "Uncle Oliver! Uncle Oliver!" cut through the sharp air. His brothers gave him a wave.

Oliver trotted up the steps of the temple and sat on one of the folded plaid blankets someone had brought to prevent them from having to sit on the cold stone.

With a smile, he watched the older children whizzing around the pond.

As he pulled on his ice skates and laced them up, he could see the manor in the distance, and he smiled to himself. As far as the eye could see, the land belonged to the Chesterfield family. He never tired of the view.

Annie came to mind, a picture of her there, beside him, smiling. Those blue eyes and that blonde hair. The image came unbidden, and it startled him.

"Uncle Oliver, are you coming or not?" called out his niece, Emma.

Oliver finished lacing up his skates and stood up. "I'm ready!" he called, glad for the distraction and pushing Annie to the outer recesses of his mind.

CHAPTER NINE

The Hope Springs Airport was so small you had to step outside to change your mind. Annie arrived early, only to find that Oliver's plane was late due to bad weather. She whipped off a quick text to her mother, letting her know that he'd been delayed, and browsed the paperback rack in front of the gift shop. Her family was just as excited about the prospect of meeting Oliver as they were about Rachel's wedding, which was a sad commentary on what her family thought of her personal life.

Luckily, she had yet to run into Brad since she'd arrived home for the wedding. And she'd like to keep it that way as long as possible.

She was so deep in thought over this that she didn't register Oliver approaching until he was within a few feet of her. She told herself to pay more attention. Again, she reminded herself that she was supposed to be making Brad jealous with Oliver, and she couldn't do that if she was thinking about Brad.

Oliver must have come right from work, as he wore an overcoat over his suit and he had a cashmere scarf around his neck.

"How are you, Annie?" he asked. He looked pale.

"I'm fine. How was the flight?" she asked.

He exhaled a breath as if he'd been holding it. "Bumpy."

Annie nodded in sympathy. "There's a storm front rolling in off the coast."

"I think the plane was riding along with it," he said.

"Do you have a suitcase?" she asked.

"Just my carry-on and a garment bag," he said.

"Let's collect it and I'll take you to your hotel," she said.

They made stilted small talk on the ride through town. Annie thought briefly of driving up Main Street, but she figured he wouldn't be interested in that. She didn't have the heart to tell Oliver that her family was all back at the house waiting for him to arrive so they could check him out. She didn't know if she should forewarn him or not. In the end, she decided he'd find out for himself. There was no sense in putting presumptions into his head. Best if he approached her family with an open mind and harbored no preconceived ideas.

She looked over at him in the passenger seat. It was hard to believe that Oliver Chesterfield was there in Hope Springs.

"I hope you don't mind, but my parents are expecting to meet you tonight," she said.

"Of course," Oliver said.

There was a lag, and Annie refrained from trying to fill in the empty gaps due to her nerves. She bit her lip to force herself to refrain from talking. She did not want a repeat of that disastrous dinner at Doug and Carol's two months earlier. She held herself and her tongue in check.

Oliver broke the silence. "What are you expecting from me?"

She quickly looked over at him. "I'm sorry?"

"Well, what I mean is that we're going to be spending a lot of time together. More than what we had to do at the Christmas party," he explained. "How do you want to appear?"

"Obviously as boyfriend and girlfriend." Her mind started to race.

"What am I allowed to do?"

She snapped her head toward him. "In regard to what?"

Oliver shifted uncomfortably on his side of the car. "In regard to any public displays of affection. It would look odd if we're shaking hands every time we meet."

Annie snorted and then quickly covered her mouth and nose, embarrassed. She cleared her throat and said quickly, "Let's keep it simple. We're a private couple not prone to embarrassing displays of affection."

"Okay," he said. "So we're going to be *that* kind of couple."

"What do you mean?" she asked.

"Shouldn't we be in the initial stages of passion?" he asked.

Annie felt her face redden. Was he teasing her? His expression was unreadable.

"Maybe you're used to women dropping at your feet," she said through gritted teeth, "but I can assure you that I always act like a lady."

Oliver stuttered, "I-I didn't mean any offense, Annie. I was only being flippant."

"I don't know you well enough to know when you're being flippant," she shot back.

"At least we've got the arguing down like a real couple," he said, staring out the window.

Annie sagged in her seat. "I'm nervous."

"What are you nervous about?" he asked.

"Everything," she admitted.

"It's just a wedding, and I promise you I won't do anything that would embarrass you," he said. "I won't stand up from the table with my napkin tucked into my pants. I won't insult your Aunt Betty. And I will help you make your ex-boyfriend jealous."

Annie laughed, the tension leaving her. "I actually have an Aunt Betty and whatever you do, please don't insult her. She's cooking the food for the reception."

Oliver grinned. "Duly noted."

The Milton Arms was bustling by the time Annie pulled in. Oliver took his garment bag and carry-on in with him while Annie parked the car. The snow was falling softly, the snowflakes appearing as if they were the most delicate things in the world. Annie watched them for a few minutes, mesmerized.

Annie loved Christmas, and she was looking forward to Rachel's wedding. But the thought of Oliver underfoot made her nervous. She had to rein that in. To be constantly hypervigilant about what she was saying would be exhausting. She glanced at the dashboard clock. She planned to take Oliver over to her parents' house, watch him like a hawk, and after a short but suitable period of time, bring him back to his hotel and not see him until the morning. She was even going to encourage him to eat his breakfast at the hotel, suggesting they'd be too occupied at the house with wedding preparations.

She'd just put her hand on the door handle when the passenger door opened, startling her, and Oliver leaned in.

"They don't have a reservation in my name," he said.

"What?" Annie said.

"There's no reservation in my name," Oliver repeated. "You did look after that, didn't you? You said you would."

Annie stared through the windshield but said nothing. "Uh . . ." She squeezed her eyes shut. His hotel reservation; she'd forgotten all about it. Instead of writing it down like she should have done, she'd thought she'd just remember it.

"Get in, Oliver," Annie said in resignation. How did she forget to make a reservation for him? The most important thing for her was him not being underfoot twenty-four-seven. And she could almost guarantee that he'd prefer a hotel room. "I'm sorry, it must have slipped my mind."

Oliver didn't say anything, and Annie couldn't tell whether he was angry or not. She hoped not. They would not be off to a great start if they arrived at her parents' house tense and angry. It would be tough to convince her family that they were in love.

Once he placed his gear in the backseat, he climbed into the front and buckled up.

"I am sorry, Oliver, I just forgot about it," she said.

"Don't worry about it," he said easily. "Hopefully, I'll be able to get a room at another hotel."

"Uh, well, that's a problem." She looked over at him. "That's the only hotel in town."

Oliver tilted his head to one side and stared at her. He sighed. "Now what?"

"You can stay at our house," she said quickly. She certainly didn't want him to worry about where he'd be sleeping.

"Won't you mind?" he asked.

"No, not at all," she said with forced cheerfulness.

She started the car and pulled out of the hotel parking lot. She had no one to blame but herself. His hotel reservation should have been the most important thing on her to-do list, not making silly wedding favors.

The ride to her parents' house was quiet and Annie didn't even bother with small talk. *He must think I'm an idiot.*

Oliver broke the silence.

"What is the agenda for the next few days?"

"Tonight, it's just the family at my parents' house. Tomorrow is the rehearsal dinner. And then, of course, the wedding the day after."

"Sounds perfect," he said.

Does it? She wondered. "Do you like weddings?"

Oliver nodded. "I do. They're brilliant—except when they're not."

CHAPTER TEN

Oliver was curious to meet Annie's family. As lovely as her mother had sounded on the phone, she'd been inquisitive, and peppered him with questions more rapid than machine-gun fire.

He'd decided he would keep things vague about his background. No one needed to know that he was the youngest son of the Duke of Chesterfield. It had been his experience that once people found out about his heritage and history, there was usually a subsequent shift in their attitude toward him. He just wanted to be treated like everyone else. It was different back home because he moved in those social circles but here, in America, he'd wanted to expand his horizons.

No one in the office knew about his background. Not even Mr. Hardcastle knew him as Lord Chesterfield. They simply knew him as Oliver. He'd worked hard to get by on his merit and he didn't want any special favors simply because of his birthright.

But he was grateful that he had someplace to go for Christmas. He would have hated to spend the holiday alone. How dreadful would that have been? And how generous of Mrs. Beasley to invite him. He looked forward to seeing how an American family celebrated Christmas.

Nearly every shop in Hope Springs was decorated in Christmas lights. Snowbanks lined the edge of the sidewalks and people walked along, their arms laden with shopping bags. It seemed like a nice little town.

It was a slight inconvenience to be out of a hotel room, but the staff at the hotel had told him they were all booked up due to Christmas and a wedding in town. Oliver couldn't believe Annie had forgotten to book him a room. How hard could it be? He partly blamed himself. He should have double-checked with her. Better yet, he should have booked it himself. He stared out the window at the passing town and sighed, determined to make the best of it.

Annie's parents lived just outside of town in a renovated farmhouse. The next house was a hundred yards away, and all Oliver could make out was a small square window of light. The long driveway of the Beasley home was packed with cars. Every window in the house was lit up. Red and green floodlights illuminated the house and the surrounding fields.

When he stepped out of Annie's car, the air was cold and damp. His breath came out in white puffs. From the house, he could hear music. There was definitely a party going on.

Carrying his garment bag over his shoulder and with his carry-on trailing behind him, Oliver followed Annie. He no sooner stepped foot on the porch than the front door flew open and a couple, whom he presumed to be Annie's parents, stood beaming at them. A crowd was packed behind them, all pressing up against each other.

"Come in, come in," Mrs. Beasley said, her smile broad.

Oliver stepped into the front hall and was engulfed in the swarm of people. He didn't know where to look first.

"Mr. and Mrs. Beasley," he said with a smile, extending his hand.

"Now, there's none of that," said Mrs. Beasley. Her hair was the color of a dried orange and she wore a Christmas sweater with ornaments, candy canes, and Christmas trees all over it. "I insist you call us by our first names, Peggy and Malcolm," she gushed.

She took him by the hand and pulled him into a big embrace. "In our family, we hug!"

Awkwardly, he put his arms around her. He'd forgotten about the tendency of Americans to be demonstrative. And the thought of calling her by her first name was unusual; his mother would have had an apoplectic stroke if she knew he was calling Mrs. Beasley by her Christian name.

Mr. Beasley extended his hand, and Oliver was relieved to see he wasn't a hugger like his wife.

"So, you're the fella Annie's been dating," he said.

Oliver wasn't able to read his tone. And he was reminded that *this* was the whole purpose of his being here. It had nothing to do with having somewhere to go for Christmas, although that was a nice advantage.

"That's right, it's great to finally meet you," he said. "And I'm to pass on Mr. Hardcastle's thanks for repairing his watch. He was chuffed."

Mr. Beasley beamed. "It was nothing. It's not a job if you love what you do."

Peggy Beasley elbowed her way in between Oliver and her husband. "All this time, Annie's been hiding you in the closet! Well, guess what, Oliver, it's time to come out of the closet!"

Oliver shuffled on his feet and Malcolm Beasley cleared his throat. He frowned with a nod toward Oliver's luggage. "Have you not checked in?"

Annie spoke up. "Um, well, that's a funny story."

Oliver thought it was a lot of things but funny wasn't one of them.

"I forgot to book Oliver's hotel reservation and he has no room," Annie said.

Peggy twittered. "No room at the inn—that's a familiar theme this time of year."

Laughter spread through the crowd.

"Remember when I asked you to stay here? It's as if it's meant to be," Peggy declared.

Oliver didn't know about that, but he expressed his gratitude.

Peggy waved him away. "Staying in a hotel at Christmas is not right."

"I don't want to put you to any trouble," Oliver said.

"It's no trouble at all," Peggy insisted. "We've got plenty of room. The more, the merrier, I always say."

And that was settled. His garment bag and carry-on were snatched from him and passed along like they were bodies in a mosh pit, until they landed at the staircase.

They all remained in the hall as Oliver and Annie removed their coats. Those were taken, too, by a pair of hands, and disappeared.

"Nice to meet you," he said for what must have been the hundredth time as relatives and friends approached him. Some hugged, others shook his hand vigorously. Oliver couldn't remember all the names. There were so many.

"Everyone, why don't we head back into the front parlor," Peggy announced. "Let Grandma and Grandpa get through first."

The crowd parted like the red sea and a tiny, elderly woman slumped over a walker slowly made her way through, en route to the parlor. She was followed by a man roughly the same age but robust in appearance with a mop of white hair and chomping on an unlit cigar. Everyone waited patiently for them. When they reached Oliver and Annie, the woman stopped and peered up at Oliver.

"Not bad looking. I'll talk to you in a minute," she said, and nodded toward the parlor. "I want to get a good seat."

Oliver nodded and smiled.

The old man stuck out his hand. "I'm Cornelius Beasley, but everyone calls me Connie. Or Grandpa Beasley, whichever you prefer."

Annie turned to Oliver. "Did you want to go upstairs and freshen up? Take a nap, maybe? You must be tired after your flight. You could even go straight to bed if you wanted. I'll see you at breakfast. Don't worry about it. I'll make excuses for you . . ."

Oliver studied her. Why was she so nervous about him being there? Was it him or was it her family that had her on edge? Or the combination of the two?

He reached out for Annie's hand, gave it a gentle squeeze, and smiled at her. There was a look of surprise on her face before it disappeared. He did not let go of her hand as they followed her father into the parlor.

The parlor was a big room with a fireplace, and there was a mishmash of furniture all over the place. No definitive style, mainly American garage sale.

A voice cut through the din of conversation. "Come sit here by me, young man."

Oliver's gaze followed the direction of the voice and landed on Grandma Fischer, sitting in a recliner. Next to her, in the other recliner, sat Grandpa Beasley.

Malcolm scratched the back of his head and whispered to Oliver, "That's Peggy's mother. It's best just to do what she asks." And with a wink, he was gone.

Oliver made his way through the crowd. He introduced himself, and Annie's grandmother narrowed her eyes at him. "My name's Frieda Fischer, but everyone calls me Grandma. Though I wish they wouldn't," she said. She took a puff from her e-cigarette.

"What would you like me to call you?"

"It depends," she said thoughtfully. "If you're just going to be a drive-by, call me Mrs. Fischer. If you're a long-termer, call me Frieda."

Oliver let out a bark of laughter. Everyone in the room looked toward him and he coughed to cover his embarrassment. Oliver sat down in the middle of the sofa across from Annie's grandparents, feeling like he was on a job interview.

"That settles it. Call me Grandma," she said. She took a long drag on her e-cigarette. "Can you believe it? After sixty years of smoking, they made me quit. It was a condition of moving in here. I'm almost ninety years old, for Pete's sake. It was that or go to a nursing home. I had no choice. But they do allow me to vape, at least. And actually, the blueberry-flavored ones are nice."

Oliver listened intently. Grandpa Beasley took over the reins of the conversation and grilled Oliver about his job, the firm, and how much rent he was paying in Manhattan.

"Stop with that, Connie," Frieda said. "Next, you'll be asking for his tax return." Grandma Fischer said no more, but she continued to watch Oliver with a mixture of curiosity and suspicion.

A young woman approached. "Oliver?"

"That's right," he said. He stood up from the couch.

"I'm Annie's sister, Rachel," she said. Oliver could see the slight resemblance but whereas Annie was blonde, Rachel was a brunette. There was an awkward moment when he went to shake her hand and she wrapped him in a hug.

"My fiancé is around here somewhere. I'd like you to meet him," she said, her eyes scanning the room. She looked back at Oliver. "You're cute. Annie never said."

Oliver was unsure if a response was warranted but responded anyway with a shrug and a smile. He glanced around the room to see if her fiancé's brother was there—Annie's ex-boyfriend. He'd like to get a good measure of him.

Not taking her eyes off him, Rachel said, "You must meet my cousin, Violet."

Before he could say anything, Rachel turned her head, lifted her hand, and waved someone over. Oliver looked up to see a young, preteen girl approach. She was smiling broadly.

Rachel made the introductions. "Oliver, this is Cousin Violet; Violet, this is Oliver Chesterfield, a friend of Annie's."

Oliver thought it was odd that Rachel had referred to him as a friend rather than a boyfriend, but said nothing.

Rachel spoke. "Cousin Violet has been to England twice with her parents, Uncle Al and Aunt Betty."

Oliver nodded and Rachel and Violet sat down on either end of the sofa with Oliver sandwiched in the middle. After some general conversation, Rachel jumped up. "Excuse me, but I must mingle." She took a step and then paused. "You know, I just had a thought. Annie is going to be pretty busy over the next two days, being the maid of honor and all. Maybe you, Violet, can look after Oliver." She raised her eyebrows and stared at her cousin.

"I'd love to," Violet said, clapping her hands.

Oliver felt as if he was being pawned off. And what did it say about him that they felt he needed childminding by a twelve-year-old?

"You're from England," Violet said, starting off the conversation.

"I am," Oliver said.

"I love England! I've been there twice," Violet said, her eyes sparkling.

"Have you? What do you like about it?" he asked, amused by her enthusiasm.

"Just about everything," she answered. "The black cabs, the tea, and anything to do with the royal family."

Oliver hesitated, not wanting to uncover a landmine in relation to his own background or heritage. He shifted the conversation to her education and asked her questions about school.

It wasn't long before her parents called her over. "Violet! Come give us hand."

Violet bounced up. "I better see what they want. Don't go anywhere, Oliver. I'll be right back."

Oliver gave a slight nod and said, "Of course."

His eyes landed on Grandma Fischer who said with a grin, "Violet's not lying. She will be right back. Now might be the time to mingle."

Oliver smiled and stood up from the sofa, and Grandma Fischer winked at him.

He circulated, introducing himself to Annie's family and friends. His gaze bounced around the room in search of Annie, but she was nowhere to be seen. He had not seen her in a while. Briefly, he wondered if she was avoiding him, but his thoughts were interrupted when he was flagged down by a family member, a retired surgeon whose name escaped Oliver. They had an earnest conversation comparing the healthcare systems of the US and the UK.

Grandpa Beasley appeared, leaning heavily on his cane. "Oliver, may I ask you a question?"

"Of course."

"How are the cigars in England?"

"Very good, if you like smoking cigars. Goes nice with a glass of port."

Grandpa Beasley smiled. "I like the sound of that."

"Will I bring you a box back the next time I'm in England?" Oliver asked.

"I wouldn't want to cause any trouble."

"It's no trouble at all," he said, making a mental note. Even though he and Annie would be going their separate ways after Christmas, there was no reason he couldn't bring back a box of cigars for her grandfather.

"I better get back to my chair before someone takes it," Grandpa Beasley said. He slapped Oliver on the arm. "Thanks, my friend."

A blonde woman with green eyes stopped him and forced a glass of mulled wine on him. She was dressed in vibrant colors of blue, green, and turquoise. "We are so happy that Annie found someone," she said. A shadow passed over her face. "She was just heartbroken when her relationship with Brad ended."

"Was she?" he asked, interested in learning more.

The woman nodded, her feathered earrings jiggling against her neck. "After five years, he decided he *needed* to travel the world. By himself." She shook her head. "Very selfish person." She nodded toward Rachel, who was standing with a man. "Luckily, his brother, Brian, seems to be a nice young man."

They spoke for a few more minutes and Oliver learned that she was a hairdresser in town and had been divorced for years. She laughed and said, "But I'm still hopeful! I just haven't met him yet."

Annie appeared at his side, and Oliver broke into a smile. "Hello there."

"I better pass the rest of these out," the relative said, referring to her tray of mulled wine.

Annie laid a hand on his arm. "Oliver, I'm so sorry. I've been in the kitchen, heating appetizers. But I'm on a union-mandated break right now," she said. She was so pretty that for a moment he wished she was his real girlfriend so he could lean in and kiss her. The urge was great.

"I see you've met everyone," Annie said.

Oliver nodded. "You've got a big family."

Everyone was in good form and after a while, Oliver didn't think he could eat another bite or drink any more eggnog or mulled wine. Uncle Al had offered him something stronger, but he had politely refused.

Peggy entered the room with a couple of bottles of champagne and announced, "Let's raise a glass to the new couple!"

When everyone was given a plastic glass of champagne, Malcolm lifted his in the air. "First, a toast to our daughter Rachel and her fiancé, Brian, who are getting married in two days! Long lives and much happiness," he said.

There was a chorus of "hear, hear" and everyone drained their glasses.

By midnight, the crowd was beginning to thin. People went out to brush off their cars and warm them up. After meeting what felt like half the town of Hope Springs, Oliver had difficulty keeping his eyes open. He yawned uncontrollably.

"Oh, Oliver, did you want to go to bed?" Peggy asked, finally sitting herself down on the sofa. Oliver didn't think he'd seen her sit all night. She was amazing, making sure everyone had something to eat or drink.

"I don't want to be rude . . ." he said, his voice trailing off.

"Of course he wants to go to bed, Peggy," Grandma Fischer said. "He must be exhausted. I know I am, and I'm related to half the people here. Why you had to have all these people over tonight is beyond me. We're going to be seeing all of them tomorrow and the next day at the wedding!"

"All right, Mother, stay in your own lane, now," Peggy said, narrowing her eyes.

Frieda grumbled something unintelligible and took a puff off her e-cigarette. "Beware of the gong," she warned Oliver.

"Yes, beware of the gong." Grandpa Beasley laughed.

Oliver frowned at them in confusion.

"Now, Oliver, just make yourself at home. If you get hungry in the middle of the night, by all means, come down and make yourself a snack," Peggy said. "I've put you in Annie's old room. I hope that isn't a problem."

"But where will Annie sleep?" he asked, hoping her parents didn't expect them to sleep in the same room.

"She can bunk with Grandma," Peggy explained. "Annie, take Oliver upstairs. Off you go!"

Tentatively, Annie reached out and took hold of Oliver's hand and they pushed their way through the crowd, saying their good nights. Up the stairs they went, with Annie still holding his hand. Oliver decided he'd follow her anywhere.

Upstairs, there were three doors on one side of the narrow corridor and two on the opposite side. Annie pointed out the bathroom, located at the end of the hall, then stopped at the first door, her hand on the doorknob. "Now Oliver, I should warn you that since I left, my room is being used as a storage space."

"That's fine," he said.

She opened the door and Oliver followed her in. He might have noticed the white princess furniture or the daisy-print wallpaper or the pink chenille bedspread on the single bed. But he couldn't, because of the mountain of paper towels and toilet paper.

Annie caught his line of sight. "My mother never met a sale she didn't like." She stood in the middle of the room and looked around. "Just make yourself comfortable. If you need an extra blanket, there's one in the closet."

He hoped he wouldn't need one, because there was no way he'd be able to get to the closet. In front of it was stacked all sorts of canned and boxed goods.

"Tomorrow we have the rehearsal dinner. I'm going to be busy getting some last-minute things ready for the wedding. I am so sorry, Oliver."

He shrugged, picking up a can from the stack. Cream of mushroom soup. He scrunched up his nose. It sounded awful. "Annie, don't worry about me. I can entertain myself. To be honest, I've brought some work with me."

Annie's posture relaxed. "We can do something, I promise."

"Not necessary, really," he said. She'd be busy enough. He didn't want to add to it.

"Oh, okay," she said, her voice tinged with uncertainty.

They both stood there. Oliver looked around the room. Annie stepped back. "Well, have a good night. I hope you'll be comfortable."

"I will be."

Annie hesitated at the door as if she wanted to say something else. Or do something. Usually, a couple kissed good night, but Oliver wasn't going to presume anything. Besides, he reminded himself, they weren't really a couple. She gave him a small smile and closed the door behind her.

Oliver stood in the middle of Annie's childhood bedroom and looked around. A framed photo of Germany's most famous castle, Neuschwanstein castle, adorned one wall. On the desk was a beer stein. He popped the lid to discover a treasure of buttons and coins. There was a pile of loose papers, mostly recipes, all in German. His glance drifted toward the dry and canned goods piled high throughout the room and he decided if there was ever an apocalypse, this would be his destination.

He lay awake for the better part of an hour, listening to the strange noises and sounds of the unfamiliar house. He tossed and turned in the narrow bed, his feet practically hanging over the end of it. He looked around the room, trying to picture teenage Annie in it. It was frilly, girly, and feminine and yet somehow, he was reassured by these things. Not so much, though, about the ceiling-high stack of paper towels.

He had just fallen into a deep sleep when he was awakened by the gong of a clock that reverberated throughout the house. The floorboards rattled. Oliver sat bolt upright in bed. "What the—"

Accidentally, he bumped into the precariously stacked paper towels next to the bed. They cascaded down upon him. Oliver, half asleep, batted them away with one arm. He glanced at them, scattered all over the floor, and decided he'd deal with it in the morning.

Chapter Eleven

The following morning, Annie arrived downstairs at breakfast to find everyone already there, including Oliver. Her mother had just set a plate of eggs and bacon down in front of him, and her father was walking around, filling everyone's cup with coffee.

As she walked in, her mother was asking Oliver a question. "Have you made any chumps in the city?"

Oliver frowned. "I beg your pardon?"

"I'm sorry, I didn't realize I was as tired as I was," Annie said, slipping into the empty seat next to Oliver. She whispered to him, "She means chums."

"Oh," Oliver said with a nod. "Yes, I have met a few people through work."

"My darling girl, you tossed and turned all night long," Grandma Fischer said.

Annie winced. "Sorry, Grandma."

Grandma gave her a dismissive wave of the hand. "You're working too hard, that's what the problem is."

Annie couldn't dispute that. She turned to Oliver, who lowered his voice, smiled, and said, "Good morning." The way he said it made Annie feel as if they were the only two people in the room.

Annie smiled shyly at him. She felt guilty for leaving him alone for most of the previous evening and she wanted to make it up to him.

"What are your plans today?" Peggy asked.

Annie looked at Oliver and said, "I'm going to help Rachel with whatever needs to be done." Feeling bad for having to leave Oliver to fend for himself, she asked, "Would you like to do something later this afternoon?"

"Only if you have time, Annie," he answered. "Don't worry about me."

"Why don't you take him ice skating? Do you skate?" Malcolm asked.

"I do, as a matter of fact," Oliver said.

"Annie, I will need your help with some last-minute arrangements," Rachel said. "We need to go and check on the flowers and review the head count one more time. Ooh, and we need to stop by the Bristol Manor to see how things are progressing from their end."

Annie stared at her and then looked at Oliver, torn.

Peggy jumped in. "Rachel, I can do those things with you. Leave Annie to spend some time with Oliver."

"No offense, Mom, but I wanted to spend some time with my maid of honor." Rachel began to pout, which was something Annie hadn't seen her do since she was six.

"Look, it's all right," Oliver said. "I've brought work with me and if you can set me up somewhere, I have plenty to keep me busy."

"Oh, Oliver," Annie said, uncertain. He had certainly not signed up for this.

"Aw, thanks, Oliver!" Rachel announced, beaming.

Despite his reassurances, Annie felt awful abandoning him. But once they got him set up in the dining room and gave him the password to the Wi-Fi, Oliver opened his laptop and pulled files from his briefcase. It looked like he'd be busy for a while.

Peggy said as they were going out the door, "Don't worry, I'll look after Oliver. I'll make sure he's fed and watered."

"Thanks, Mom," Annie said, heading out of the house and following Rachel to her car.

As Rachel pulled out of the driveway, she chatted excitedly about her big day. Despite her misgivings about abandoning Oliver, Annie had to admit that it was wonderful to see Rachel so happy.

Rachel's high-school pal had done a fabulous job with the flowers, and after they left her house, Annie got to thinking about what kind of flowers she'd like for her own wedding. An image of her walking down the aisle holding a bouquet in front of her filled her head. But it was the image of Oliver standing at the altar, waiting for her, that unnerved her. She gave her head a shake.

"I thought we could meet Brian for lunch," Rachel suggested.

"Sure," Annie said. She'd only had toast at breakfast and her stomach was starting to growl. "We can swing by and pick up Oliver."

Rachel had an odd expression on her face.

"What?" Annie said.

"It might be nice if it was just us," Rachel said.

"Oh, like a sister thing?" Annie asked. She was all for that. She glanced at her watch. Maybe a quick lunch, she thought. She didn't like being gone too long from Oliver. It wasn't fair.

"Well, no, Brian, too," Rachel said.

"Okay, that's fine. Let's pick up Oliver, too," Annie said, going back to her original plan.

Rachel hesitated. "I meant me, you, Brian, and Brad. You know, the bride and groom, maid of honor and best man."

"No," Annie said firmly. "I do not want to go to lunch with my ex-boyfriend."

"It's just the four of us."

Annie looked over at her, wondering why her sister would think this was all right. "Go to lunch with my ex-boyfriend while my boyfriend waits at our house? Um, I don't think so." She glanced at her watch again, even though she knew the time. "Actually, I've been gone long enough. Take me home."

Rachel was sullen behind the steering wheel. But Annie didn't care. She didn't know what Rachel was up to but she knew she didn't like it.

There was silence on the ride and by the time they reached the house, both girls were in a sour mood.

When they arrived at the restaurant for the rehearsal dinner, Annie was relieved to see there was valet parking. She did not treasure the thought of traipsing through an icy parking lot wearing high heels. As Annie pulled up to the entrance, she spotted Brad standing there. She steeled herself for their initial meeting.

Her mood had improved considerably as the afternoon wore on. This was all about Rachel's big day and they should be happy, and Annie wasn't going to let a silly squabble ruin it or come between them. A week from now, she'd never see either Oliver or Brad again.

As they approached the steps, Oliver handed a folded bill to Brad.

Brad frowned. "Do you think you're funny?"

Oliver's face was awash in confusion. "Excuse me? Aren't you the valet?"

Annie had to suppress a giggle. The expression on Brad's face was priceless. It was a mixture of pure offense, confusion, and scrambling for a comeback.

She looped her arm through Oliver's. "No, Oliver, this is Brad."

Oliver swung his head around at Annie and lowered his voice. "Brad? *Your* Brad?"

Aware that Brad's eyes were on her, Annie rambled, "He's not *my* Brad. He hasn't been for a long time. It was his choice, of course—"

Oliver took her hand in his and gave it a gentle squeeze. He smiled at her reassuringly. Annie took a deep breath and calmed down.

Brad stepped forward and kissed Annie on her cheek. "You look great, Annie." He acknowledged Oliver with a nod but said nothing to him.

Annie made the introductions. "Brad, this is my boyfriend, Oliver Chesterfield. Oliver, this is Brad Hobart."

Brad peered at Oliver as he shook his hand. The valet approached, and Annie handed him the car keys while Oliver tipped him.

There was an awkward silence before Oliver looked at Annie and said, "We'd better get you inside, darling, before you freeze to death." With a backward glance at Brad, he said over his shoulder, "Nice to have met you."

Darling? How British! And how perfect! Annie thought. As they walked away, Oliver placed his hand on the small of her back, and every nerve ending in Annie's body hummed.

The families of the bride and groom were having a drink in the bar before dinner. Oliver was immediately swallowed up by the Beasley family.

Annie stepped back and her heel landed on someone's foot. Horrified, she turned around and came face-to-face with Brad.

"Oh!" she said, immediately taking a step back.

"How are you, Annie?" he said, grinning. "There wasn't a chance to talk with you outside." He looked around and scratched the back of his head. "It's crazy how we're going to be related by marriage."

Annie would call it a lot of things. Maybe inconvenient. Unfortunate. But not crazy. Brad looked good, but then he always did. Her chest hurt. She had been dreading this meeting, but she'd known it was inevitable. She couldn't avoid him forever. Maybe it was best to get it over with.

"I guess," she said lamely. Was that the best she had? Her objective was to prove that she had moved on, survived, been happy despite everything. She stood straighter and smiled.

"How's the big city?" he asked.

"It's great, I love it," she enthused, hoping it wasn't too much.

"You seem to have landed on your feet," he said.

Annie wasn't sure whether he was referring to their breakup or in general.

"So that's your new boyfriend," Brad said.

Annie looked over at Oliver. He was whispering something in Grandma Fischer's ear, and Grandma laughed and hit him lightly on the arm. Violet stood with them, looking up at Oliver with a look of pure adoration on her face.

"It is," Annie said softly.

"Yeah," Brad said. His tone was dismissive, which Annie took as a positive. Maybe their ruse would work after all.

Not wanting to talk too much about Oliver or her personal life, Annie asked, "How are you? How was the traveling? Are you still living in Hope Springs?"

He laughed. "Still with all the questions."

Annie's smile faltered. She'd forgotten about how Brad used to say she asked too many questions. Her first meeting with Oliver had gone disastrously for the same reason. Maybe she wasn't meant to have a partner.

"Hey, relax, I was just joking," he said, laying his hand on her arm.

She shifted her position so he would have to remove his hand.

"But yeah, I backpacked through South America for six months." His expression filled with wonder. In all the years they'd been together, he'd never looked at her like that. "It was amazing."

"I bet it was," Annie said.

"But here I am back in Hope Springs, working for my dad again," Brad said, referring to his father's lumber company.

"Where are you off to next?" she asked.

He shrugged and grinned. "I don't know yet. Wherever the wind leads me."

She remembered that about Brad, too. His affected go-with-the-flow attitude. It used to make her head spin.

"Well, it was good seeing you," Annie said, stepping away.

Brad put up his arms, palms up. "That's it? I want to do some catching up with you, Annie."

"Another time, maybe," she said, taking another step away.

"All right, but you owe me one conversation," he said, pointing at her and grinning.

When she turned around, she found herself gritting her teeth. *Old habits die hard*, she thought. She didn't owe him a thing. As she blended into the group, inching closer to Oliver, she realized that her first meeting with Brad since their breakup had gone better than she'd expected. She'd thought she'd be teary, hopeful, happy to see him, but she was none of these things. She stopped mid-step and examined how she felt. She felt nothing, except for the relief of that first meeting being over with. Ambivalent, that's how she felt.

And if she could help it, she would not be having a conversation with him. Why would he want one, anyway? They'd had no contact for the past year. Unless he wanted to tell her all about his amazing backpacking experience in the Southern Hemisphere. That had been the thing that had wounded her. When he was dumping her, he told her how he wanted to experience new things and that would involve some traveling around the world. He'd known of her desire to travel the world, had known it since their first date. Desperate to hang on to her relationship with him, she'd said she would leave her job and travel with him. She'd go wherever he wanted to go. When he rejected her offer to accompany him, she realized he wanted to travel, just not with her. That had been eye opening.

The whole experience had turned on its head what she believed about herself, her life, her relationship, and most of all, her future. Within months of the breakup, she had accepted a job in the city and headed off, much to the surprise of her family and friends.

And it was at that moment, standing in front of a crowded bar packed with her family, that Annie realized she was no longer in love with Brad. When she had stopped loving him, she didn't know. Maybe it was when he left her. But it didn't matter. The only thing that mattered was that she no longer loved him. The relief of that realization made her want to weep.

From across the room, she watched Oliver amid her family, getting along with them, teasing Grandma about something and getting a laugh out of her. There was a hum of merry conversation that floated among them and Annie felt happy. At this moment, she was content. As she twirled her drink in her hands, she continued to study Oliver. If she was honest, she could not find fault with him. For someone who was supposed to be only pretending to be her boyfriend, he sure had gone to a lot of trouble. What was not to like about him? He was a dream come true.

Annie maneuvered her way through the crowd until she reached Oliver. Violet was telling Oliver about the queen's diet and what Her Majesty ate every day. Annie slipped her hand into Oliver's. He looked down at her and smiled. When she looked up, she caught Brad staring at her from across the room. She leaned against Oliver and smiled up at him. Oliver did not let go of her hand.

By the time Annie and Oliver sat down for dinner across the table from Uncle Al, Aunt Betty, and Violet, Annie began to indulge in the fantasy that Oliver really was her boyfriend. Playing the part of his girlfriend was proving to be easy.

The restaurant was called the Olde English Pub and Annie worried that it might be too kitschy for Oliver's taste. It was a Tudor-style restaurant with old portraits donning the walls. The ceilings were low, which Annie thought gave it a claustrophobic feeling. But if he had a negative opinion of the place, he didn't let on.

The starters were served, and Aunt Betty sniffed at it and scrunched up her nose. "Oh, Al, they've used too much garlic." She pursed her lips and shook her head. Annie didn't want to say too much. They all had their fingers crossed for the one hundred and fifty dinners Uncle Al and Aunt Betty would be preparing for the wedding.

"What's on the menu for tomorrow night?" Annie asked.

"Oh, it's going to be a surprise," Uncle Al said with a wink.

"Oh, I bet it will be," she said. She had tried to talk to her mother again about the arrangements but her mother held firm, saying she couldn't disappoint her sister and besides, there would be enough desserts for the midnight coffee-and-tea station that if the dinner was a total disaster, people could fill up on Christmas bars and cookies.

"We're hoping to kick off our new catering business with Rachel's wedding," Uncle Al said.

"Really? Another one?" Annie said.

"If at first you don't succeed . . ." Uncle Al laughed and took a bite of his starter. He frowned and said to his wife, "You're right, way too much garlic. Maybe we should go back to the kitchen and show them how to cook."

Annie paled.

"Uncle Al, Aunt Betty, tell us about your last trip to England," she said, changing the subject to prevent them from charging off to the kitchen.

Aunt Betty's face lit up. "We loved it." She turned to Violet. "We had a great time, honey, didn't we?"

The younger girl agreed. "It was awesome!"

"For this trip, we did a tour of some of England's great manor houses," Uncle Al chimed in.

Oliver shifted slightly in his seat. Annie gave him a quick smile, puzzled by the odd expression on his face.

"That must have been wonderful," Annie enthused. It was something she wouldn't mind seeing herself. Oliver offered no comment.

Violet spoke up. "Remember that one estate in Somerset? Dimples?" She broke into a fit of girlish giggles.

Aunt Betty laughed. "This estate was fabulous. They had a small Greek temple outside and a pond that the family used for ice skating in the winters. But anyway, I digress. The amazing thing was when we looked at the portraits of the ancestors, *all* the men had dark hair and dimples!"

"Oliver looks just like them, doesn't he, Mommy?" Violet asked.

Aunt Betty glanced at Oliver and tilted her head to one side.

Oliver looked down at his plate of food.

Now Violet stared at Oliver, her smile disappearing. Annie looked from her aunt to her cousin to Oliver and wished they would let her in on whatever secret they were sharing.

Violet's eyes widened and she asked, her voice almost a whisper, "Oliver, are you related to them? Chesterfield was the name of the family and their estate. I have it written in my scrapbook."

"Don't be ridiculous, Violet," her mother said.

As Violet and her mother went back and forth, Annie noticed that Oliver had remained unusually quiet. She cocked an eyebrow.

Finally, Aunt Betty asked, "Oliver, are you? I know it's a long shot, but hey, you never know unless you ask."

Annie laughed at their preposterous idea but when she looked at Oliver and saw his face devoid of any kind of reaction, she stopped.

All eyes were on Oliver.

"The Duke of Chesterfield is my father," he said simply.

Annie's mouth fell open, as did Aunt Betty's and Uncle Al's. Violet clapped her hands and shrieked, causing everyone at the far end of the table to turn and look their way.

Annie almost said, "Really?" but quickly stopped herself. Wouldn't she already know this information about her boyfriend?

"Will you someday be the duke?" Aunt Betty asked.

"No, that title will go to my oldest brother," Oliver explained.

"Are you a lord?" Uncle Al asked.

"Um, yes." Oliver fidgeted with the stem of his wine glass, not looking at anyone.

Annie stared at him. She didn't know whether she felt surprised or angry. He could have at least told her. *Lord Chesterfield, huh?* She grabbed her water goblet and took a large gulp.

Uncle Al slapped his thigh. "I don't believe this! We've got royalty in our midst. Well done, Annie!"

"Did you know your boyfriend was the son of a duke?" Aunt Betty asked.

"Oh sure, that's what attracted me to him," Annie said breezily with a laugh, although nothing felt funny. "I mean seriously, I've watched enough *Downton Abbey* to know I want to end up upstairs and not downstairs."

"Oh, Annie, you're so bad." Her aunt laughed.

Annie prattled on, unable to look at Oliver. She felt as if a rug had been pulled out from under her. He could have told her. What was the big secret?

It soon passed all around the wedding party and from table to table that Oliver was Lord Chesterfield, the son of a duke. Family members began to lob questions like grenades at him.

"What does your father do? Other than counting his money?"

"Do you have your own valet? I wouldn't mind one of those myself!"

"Why do you work if you don't have to?"

And finally, from Grandma Fischer, "I don't see what the big deal is. He puts his shoes and socks on one at a time like the rest of us." Oliver had laughed at this.

Annie stood up from the table and laid her napkin down. "Excuse me, I need the restroom."

Oliver followed her out a moment later. Once they were out of the room and out of earshot of everyone else, he called out, "Annie, wait up."

Annie stopped and turned around to face him, her arms folded across her chest.

"Look, I'm sorry you had to find out that way, but I don't tell anyone who I am," he said.

"Why not?"

"Because I want to be judged on my own merit and not because of my family, my background, or my heritage."

"You couldn't tell me? Confide in me?" Annie said.

Oliver sighed. "May I be blunt?"

"What, do I have lipstick on my teeth again?" she asked.

Oliver frowned. He lowered his voice. "Honestly, that detail was not necessary to our arrangement."

Annie's face reddened. She felt as if she'd just been slapped. "Very well, my lord."

Oliver grimaced. "Please don't be like that."

"As you said, it's strictly an arrangement and your personal life is none of my business," she said coolly. How could she ever have found him attractive? He was arrogant. Haughty. He was every stereotype she had of wealthy people.

"Look, I'm sorry, Annie. If it's any consolation, the firm doesn't even know. I earned that position. It had nothing to with who I was or who I knew. I didn't want to use my father's connections from his years in the diplomatic service, and I wanted to step out of my older brothers' shadows. It was important to me to do it on my own. That's why I came to America, because no one knows me here, and I can be myself."

Annie's expression softened. A part of her could understand that. She sighed. "I just wish you would have trusted me."

"I wish I had too. I realize my mistake with bitter regret," he said. "What about the rest of your family?" He glanced back toward the dining room.

"Can't help you there. By tomorrow, the whole town will know. Be glad that they don't live in the city," she said.

Oliver laughed. "All right, I will be glad for that."

"Are there any more secrets that I need to know? I don't like to be blindsided. I can't pretend to be your girlfriend if I don't know anything about you. I mean, as it stands, my aunt and uncle knew more about you than I did," Annie said, glancing around to make sure no one was in earshot.

"There's nothing else," he said.

They began to walk in the general direction of the restrooms.

"So, am I to call you 'my lord' and all that? Are you expecting me to curtsy?" Annie asked, looking up at him.

Oliver grinned. "Only if you want to."

Annie elbowed him and smirked. "Don't push your luck, Lord Chesterfield."

By the time they returned to the Beasley family home, the entire family on both sides knew all about Oliver's background. As a result, he was bombarded with questions. Annie felt sorry for him. It had slightly changed her perception of him. Before, he was just Oliver from the building she worked in, but now . . .

Immediately, she could understand why he didn't want people to know; she could understand his need to level the playing field. She watched as he interacted with her family, patiently fielding their questions. Boy, they were a nosy bunch.

They ended up in the living room with Oliver squished on the sofa between Peggy and Aunt Betty. Violet perched on the arm of Grandma Fischer's chair, and Annie pulled up a chair to join the group.

"Have you ever been to a royal wedding?" Peggy asked.

"Which one?" Oliver asked.

Peggy and Betty raised their eyebrows.

"Any of them. Harry and Meghan? William and Kate?" Aunt Betty asked.

Oliver rubbed his forefinger along his temple. "Yes, I did attend those weddings."

Again, there was silence among the group. Even Grandma Fischer and Grandpa Beasley seemed to view him differently. They were speechless, which was nothing short of miraculous.

"Wait a minute!" Peggy jumped up from the sofa and headed to a magazine rack tucked in the corner. She dug through it and pulled out an old magazine, its glossy cover worn and tattered. "I'm so glad I saved this!" Quickly, she flipped through it, stopped at a page, and said triumphantly, "Aha!" Folding the magazine in half, she carried it back to the group.

"Look, here's a picture of Oliver at the last royal wedding," she said, handing the magazine to Aunt Betty. Both women leaned over it, studying it.

"Oh, Oliver, you look dashing in a top hat," Peggy said, studying the picture and then looking over at Oliver before passing the magazine to Grandma Fischer.

Grandma studied the magazine photo and narrowed her eyes. "Who's the girl on your arm?"

"That's my friend Phillipa," he answered.

Phillipa? Annie wondered. A girlfriend back home? He hadn't mentioned her, either. She couldn't help but feel as if someone had turned the lights out and she was left groping around in the dark.

When the magazine finally came around and landed in her lap, Annie bent her head to study the picture. Her mother had been right; Oliver cut a dashing figure. The top hat, the morning suit with the ascot tie . . . it all suggested an upper-class upbringing and a genteel lifestyle. Good breeding. Old money. Good gracious!

It dawned on her that their lives were as different from each other as possible. Their romance would seem unlikely to most. It certainly seemed unlikely to her. Any possibility of romance now seemed remote. She looked around the living room of the house she'd grown up in. The comfortable though mismatched furniture, the worn carpet, and the dated wallpaper. Suddenly, she felt embarrassed, as if she couldn't pull this off. There was no one there who could possibly believe she'd land someone as elegant as Oliver. Even Annie didn't believe it.

Annie focused on the woman on Oliver's arm. They looked like they belonged together. She was a tall, willowy brunette. In her heels, she was almost as tall as Oliver. Annie felt herself shrink in her chair. He was used to attending weddings at Buckingham Palace and Windsor Castle, and meanwhile, Annie was logging hours in her mother's kitchen, making favors for her sister's wedding. Their worlds were so far apart they might as well have been on different planets. They had nothing in common. Nothing. What made her think that Oliver could be interested in her?

Although she had no right, she would certainly question Oliver about this Phillipa later. He had not used the word "girlfriend"; maybe she was just a friend. He was so good-looking, though, that it would not be much of a stretch for him to have a girlfriend back home. And by the looks of the girl—woman—she traveled in the same circles as Oliver.

How could she ever think there could be a romance with Oliver? That he could feel about her the way she'd begun to feel about him? Had she forgotten their first meeting? She blamed Christmas. She blamed the wedding. The combination of the two had made her vulnerable. Plus, it had been a while since she dated anyone, and even though they had gotten off on the wrong foot, he had been nothing but solicitous and kind since. He'd been the *perfect* boyfriend. The whole fake relationship thing had swept her away. The lines between reality and pretend had blurred.

Annie didn't know where to look or what to do. She passed the magazine on to Grandpa Beasley. He seemed to be studying the image, as well. Would their fake relationship survive the unrelenting scrutiny? She blinked, looked around again, and fidgeted with her hands in her lap. Her gaze landed on Oliver. He was staring at her and offered her a small smile. In response, Annie sat up straighter and smiled at him. It was foolish to pine away for someone like him. What right had she to be indignant over the existence of someone named Phillipa? No right whatsoever. She could hardly be upset with him.

Then he'd know. He'd know that she found him attractive. That his accent, coupled with those smoldering eyes and his manners, were like kryptonite to her. No, he must never know, Annie decided. He'd laugh all the way back to his estate.

She looked at him, sitting there surrounded by her family in an old farmhouse full of clocks. And she decided that as much as she didn't belong in his world, he didn't belong in hers, either.

The noise that surrounded her could not drown out the thoughts zinging around her mind at a high rate of speed. And with them came the sobering realization that for the first time since Brad dumped her, she had moved on. She *liked* someone else. But it was obviously going to be a one-sided affair.

How depressing.

Chapter Twelve

If he did nothing else before he went back to the city, Oliver had to make sure Annie knew that Phillipa was just a friend. A very good friend. But he didn't want there to be any mistaken assumptions. Didn't want Annie jumping to any erroneous conclusions that he and Phillipa were romantically involved.

Oliver needed some fresh air. Not only were all of Annie's family crowded into the Beasley home but Brian's family was there as well, which included Brad. Oliver had tried to keep his eye on him and where he was in relation to Annie at all times.

He slipped out of the living room, found his coat on the stand in the front hall, and quietly went outside onto the front porch. Once he closed the door behind him, the noise and revelry became muted. He drew in a deep breath of crisp, frigid air. At first, he didn't see Brad standing there, taking a swig from a beer bottle. Oliver hesitated, but in the end, he stood his ground.

Brad smirked, all swarthy looks and thick hair, and it took all of Oliver's self-control not to knock the smug expression off his face. Oliver wondered how Annie ever ended up with this guy. She must have been having an off day.

"Just want to give you notice," Brad said, flashing brace-straightened teeth.

Oliver scowled, not comprehending. "Put me on notice?"

"I intend to win Annie back."

Oliver kept his face neutral. "Good luck."

Brad's face darkened. "I don't need luck, but you do. I don't care how much money you have or whether you're a duke or not. Annie's not that type of girl. She loves Hope Springs, and she belongs here."

Oliver wanted to laugh in his face. This guy had apparently given it some thought. And even though he didn't know what kind of future he and Annie had—it might all end as soon as they returned to New York—there was something about Brad that rankled him.

"We'll see about that," Oliver said evenly. Did he have a chance with Annie? And more importantly, did he want one?

"You're forgetting one thing," Brad said with a smile. "Annie loved me once. She can love me again." He paused and added with a chuckle, "That's if she ever stopped loving me."

The comment burrowed beneath Oliver's skin like a mite. He had to admit that logically, Brad was right. If she loved him once, she might very easily be able to love him again.

His mood began to sour.

Brad walked past him, saying nothing, which Oliver figured was just as well, considering it might lead to an altercation. Nothing would give him greater satisfaction than taking a swing at Brad, if only to wipe that smirk off his face. But he reminded himself that he didn't want to cause trouble on the eve of the wedding.

Alone, Oliver looked around the porch. There was a swing that was cleared off and he entertained the thought of sitting on it. When he was a kid, he'd wanted one, even an old tire hanging from a tree, but his mother had been dismissive and pronounced them *common*. And as he debated this internally, a car horn honked. Not once or twice but three times. Oliver looked up, peering around. In the driveway idled an older-model Cadillac in a magnificent shade of turquoise, a long boat of a car with the back end dipping down. The driver's-side window opened and a beefy hand emerged and waved him over. Curious, Oliver made his way carefully down the porch steps and walked along the shoveled path to the driveway.

As he approached, he peered in the open window and found Grandpa Beasley and Grandma Fischer sitting in the front seat, smoking cigars. Oliver grinned. These two were worse than a pair of hyperactive toddlers.

With a nod toward the backseat, Grandpa Beasley said, "Get in, Oliver."

At his invitation, Oliver climbed into the backseat of the car. Annie's family were eccentric but he had to hand it to them, they were never dull.

The interior of the car smelled like cherry cigars and it reminded him of his grandfather, long dead, and his library filled with old books and pipes, his basset hound fast asleep in front of the fire.

Grandma Beasley turned around in her seat. "Had enough? We did, too. Came out for a smoke break."

Oliver couldn't help but laugh.

"Would you like a cigar?" Grandpa Beasley asked.

"No, thank you, but don't let me stop you."

"We won't," Grandma Fischer said.

"It's a little cold out here, don't you think?" Oliver felt compelled to ask. Though it was evident by the cold puffs of air they emitted every time they spoke.

"It is a bit nippy but there are too many people in the house," Grandpa Beasley said. He sounded grumpy.

"Peggy always invites way too many people," Grandma Fischer concurred.

"And then you can't get them out of the house with a shoehorn. I want to go to bed but I feel like I have to stay downstairs until everyone leaves," Grandpa Beasley complained.

"That's why we came out here to Connie's car for a smoke," Grandma Fischer said, waving her hand toward the house, cigar smoke doing a loop in the air in front of her. "You can only take so much of this stuff." She paused and said to Grandpa Beasley, "Although I don't know why you can't pick me up a pack of cigarettes."

Grandpa Beasley took a hearty drag off his cigar. "Because. I told you, Peggy will smell cigarette smoke a mile away, whereas they're used to the cigars and they won't know we're out here smoking."

There was a companionable pause.

"I saw you speaking with Brad on the porch," Grandma Fischer said. "Don't pay attention to him, Oliver. Annie won't go back to him."

Oliver couldn't be too sure, but said nothing.

"He's not good enough for Annie anyway," she concluded.

Oliver did agree with her on that point.

Changing the subject, Grandpa Beasley asked, "What do you think of the family?"

"They're a great bunch, nice people," Oliver said truthfully.

"I wish someone someday would say, 'Nice family but they're crackers,' or 'Did you get a load of that aunt in the corner?' etc., etc." Grandma Fischer laughed.

Oliver laughed, too. Grandma Fischer called it like it was.

"Oliver, what is your intention for our Annie?" Grandpa Beasley asked. They both turned and stared at him.

Although they appeared elderly and frail, these two were sharper than most. Oliver should have known to be on guard. He coughed to buy himself some time.

"I don't know if I like the fact that you're hesitating," Grandpa Beasley said.

"Oh no, it's just that I wouldn't want to speak out of turn," Oliver said. "We haven't talked too much about our future . . . ah, um . . . together." He was being honest if maybe disingenuous. "The truth is we're still in the early stages of our relationship, and we're still getting to know one another."

"Well, what do you think so far? Will Annie become Lady Chesterfield?" Grandma Fischer said with a gleam in her eye.

Sweat broke out on his brow. These two were fast-moving, like a raging river. "As I said, we're not that far into the relationship."

"You couldn't find a nicer girl than Annie," Grandpa Beasley said. He looked at Oliver in the rearview mirror.

"I believe that to be true," Oliver said, looking toward the front porch to see if maybe there was anyone about. Anyone to rescue him from this awkward conversation.

"Of course it's true," Grandma Fischer said. "She's a wonderful girl. I pray she finds someone worthy of her." Grandma turned again toward him and asked, "Do you think that would be you? Just because you're a duke doesn't make you worthy."

Oliver squirmed in the backseat, not bothering to correct Grandma on his actual title. "In the end, I think it would be up to Annie to decide who was worthy of her," Oliver replied. He added thoughtfully, "I trust her judgment."

Grandpa Beasley laughed. "Well said, young man."

Even though the car was running and the heat was on, the back window was open and snow was blowing in. Oliver's teeth chattered. He shivered in his coat, wishing he'd brought his scarf and gloves out with him.

"Come on, we better finish up before we freeze to death," Grandma Fischer said.

"Or before Malcolm starts looking for us."

"Neither a good outcome," Grandma Fischer said.

When Oliver entered the house, he was greeted by Annie. "Where have you been?"

Oliver smiled. "I've been hanging out with your grandparents." He blew on his hands.

"Really?" she asked, looking skeptical.

"Really," he confirmed. "We had a nice long conversation about my intentions toward you."

Annie's face paled. "Oh no. They didn't."

Oliver laughed and changed the subject. "I think I'd like a hot beverage," he said, rubbing his hands, trying to get the feeling back into them.

"Come on, follow me." Annie grinned and led him back to the kitchen.

At the end of the night, Annie and Oliver headed up the staircase. The only sound was the pendulum swinging and ticking in the grandfather clock. They reached the landing, and she turned to him. "Good night, Oliver. I'll see you in the morning. We've got a long day tomorrow."

"We do," he said. Her demeanor had changed since that magazine article had been passed around. He hoped it was just fatigue.

She looked up at him with those big blue eyes and said, "Thank you for being such a great sport about all of this. It must seem overwhelming at times."

"Not at all," he said, anxious to put her at ease. "Actually, I am enjoying myself."

"It certainly won't be a royal wedding," Annie said.

"Well, thank goodness for that. Listen, Annie," he said, "I would like to clarify something. I've known Phillipa since I was four. She's a neighbor. And we tend to be each other's dates when we have weddings and other functions to go to."

"Oliver, you certainly don't owe me an explanation," she said evenly. "I haven't forgotten that this is strictly an arrangement. You are under no obligation to explain anything to me."

Oliver didn't say anything. She slipped down the hallway and into Grandma Fischer's room before he could even say good night.

As he headed to bed, he was more confused than ever.

Oliver had no sooner dozed off than he was awakened with a start. At first he thought it was the gong, but then he heard voices in the hallway and doors slamming like it was three in the afternoon instead of three in the morning.

He slipped out of bed wearing a T-shirt and pajama bottoms and felt around beneath the rolls of paper towels on the floor for his slippers. Once his feet were in his slippers, he pulled his robe off the foot of the bed and threw it on. Gingerly, he stepped over fallen paper-towel rolls and made it to the door. Once there, he opened it and stuck his head out. There were voices at the other end of the hall coming from one of the rooms. The ceiling light in the hall was on. Peggy and Malcolm came out of one of the rooms and knocked on Grandma Fischer's door, whispering, "Annie, Annie."

"Is everything all right?" Oliver asked. It couldn't be if they were knocking on Annie's door in the middle of the night to wake her up.

"Oh, Oliver, could you give us a hand?" Peggy asked. Both she and her husband wore robes over their nightwear. Peggy was clad in a flannel nightgown and Malcolm had striped pajamas on.

Oliver stepped out of his room, hoping everything was okay. At that point, Annie opened her door and said, "What's going on?"

"Grandpa fell out of bed," Peggy said.

As the four of them gathered outside Grandpa Beasley's room, Grandma Fischer stuck her head out into the hallway, hands firmly planted on her walker. "What's wrong?"

"Grandpa fell out of bed," Annie told her.

"I told him that bed was too high and to get a lower one like mine," she harrumphed. "Well, I can be of no use here. I can barely pick myself up much less a man twice my size."

"It's okay, Grandma, we'll take care of it. Go back to bed."

Grandma paused and asked, "Is he all right?"

There was laughter coming from the bedroom, and it sounded like the victim.

Grandma smirked, shook her head, and returned to her room, closing the door behind her.

Oliver followed Annie into her grandfather's room. The bedside light was on, and leaning against the bed was Grandpa Beasley, his legs splayed out, dressed in flannel pajamas. Immediately, Oliver had to agree with Grandma Fischer. The bed was too high. It was an ornately carved four-poster, antique and of good quality. Oliver tried not to look alarmed. He was lucky he hadn't been hurt. There was a single-sized mattress on the floor next to the bed; either it had happened before or they'd been preparing for it.

Peggy and Malcolm were bent over Grandpa Beasley.

"What happened, Grandpa?" Annie asked. "Are you hurt?"

Grandpa shook his head. "No, I'm fine. I was dreaming of being on the beach with your grandmother." He added hastily, "Your grandmother Beasley, not that old windbag next door."

Here, he started laughing. "And I said to your grandmother, 'I think I need to turn over, I'm getting too hot!'" He broke into peals of laughter.

"Maybe we should call an ambulance," Annie said.

Grandpa's eyes grew wide, the laughter stopped, and he roared, "I'm not going to the hospital! Those places are death traps!"

In response to the shouting, there was a series of thumps on the common wall he shared with Grandma Fischer.

He waved his hand in the direction of Grandma Fischer's room. "Calm down, woman!"

"All right, Dad, we have to get you back into bed," Malcolm said.

"Pull that chair over here," Grandpa Beasley said, pointing to the desk on the other side of the room. Oliver retrieved the chair and brought it over to him.

"Face it toward me, young man," Grandpa commanded. He got on his knees and leaned on the seat of the chair. From there Malcolm, with the help of Oliver, was able to get him into a standing position.

"Okay, Dad, let's get you into bed."

"I can do it myself," Grandpa said.

"I know."

He tried three times to get into the bed but without success. Oliver could see that it was just too high. The bed was pushed up against the other wall, which was good. At least he couldn't fall out that side. They even tried a footstool, but Grandpa Beasley was too tired to lift his leg high enough to get onto the bed.

Finally, Grandpa Beasley collapsed on the chair, breathless. He waved Malcolm over. "Come on, Malcolm, give me a hand."

Malcolm knelt by the bed and cradled his hands together for his father to put his foot into for a boost.

Peggy pushed Malcolm away. "Oh no, Malcolm. What if you throw your back out? Do you want to walk Rachel down the aisle tomorrow all stooped over like the Hunchback of Notre Dame? Oh, what was his name? Igor? Ivan?"

"Quasimodo, Mom," Annie said shortly. "Dad, Mom's right. You just got your back feeling better."

Oliver stepped up. "I can do it."

They all looked at him as if he'd just ridden in on a white horse.

Malcolm helped his father up as Oliver bent his knees and cradled his hands.

"Grandpa, put your hands on the bed for stability while Oliver boosts you in," Annie instructed.

"All right, Annie," Grandpa said.

Once he was ready, Oliver said, "Mr. Beasley, I'm going to count to three, and on three I'm going to boost you into the bed."

Oliver was a little anxious about this. He hoped he could help the elderly man. With Grandpa's slippered foot in his hands, Oliver said, "One . . . two . . . three!" And with as much force as he could manage, he boosted Grandpa Beasley. Unfortunately, Annie's grandfather was a lot lighter than he appeared, and not only cleared the bed but sailed right over it, his shoulder hitting the wall on the opposite side with a thud.

"Great Mother of God," Grandpa Beasley groaned.

Oliver was horrified. "Mr. Beasley, I am terribly sorry."

Peggy laid her hand on Oliver's arm. "He's fine. The main thing is he's in his bed."

"Mr. Beasley, are you hurt?" Oliver asked.

"I'm fine, young man," he said with a weak laugh. "But I don't think you know your own strength."

Oliver sighed. Maybe he didn't.

Annie had climbed up on the bed to reposition her grandfather and straighten him out. She pulled up the blankets and adjusted the pillows behind him. Oliver could tell that this wasn't the first time she'd done this. When she was finished, she kissed him on the forehead.

"Annie, you're a gem," Grandpa said to her.

Malcolm turned to Oliver and smiled. "It's a good thing you were here, Oliver! Thank you so much for all your help." He took Oliver's hand and shook it heartily, smiling.

They were a strange group, Annie's family. He'd just about put Grandpa Beasley through the wall and they were thanking him. It made him want to shake his head.

Once they got Grandpa tucked in for the night, he said. "I could go for a cigar right now."

"No!" Annie, her mother, and her father yelled in unison.

"It was just a thought. You don't need to be so salty!" he bit back.

"Goodnight, Grandpa," they all called as they edged out of the room and flipped off the light.

The door to Grandma Fischer's room opened and she poked her head out.

"Did you get the old coot back into bed?"

"Oliver did! Thank goodness," Peggy said. She turned to her husband. "Maybe we should get a baby monitor for Grandpa's room."

Before Malcolm could answer, Grandma Fischer said, "You so much as think about putting a baby monitor in my room and I swear, Peggy, I'll start smoking in my bed. Cigarettes!" She slammed the door.

"Oh well, it was just a thought," Malcolm said with a grin.

"Come on everyone, we've got to get back to bed, we've got a wedding tomorrow," Peggy said, clapping her hands.

Annie had her hand on the doorknob to Grandma Fischer's bedroom. She stepped away and leaned up to Oliver on her tiptoes, kissed his cheek, and smiled. "Thank you, Oliver. Good night."

Chapter Thirteen

On the morning of the wedding, Annie, Rachel, and their mother went off to the salon to get their hair done. Corners had been cut for many aspects of the day, but not this. This was Annie's treat, because she wanted her sister to feel like a million bucks on her big day. She'd also arranged for them to have manicures and pedicures and makeup. They would be there all morning.

As Annie sat in her chair on the elevated platform with her feet in a tub of swirling water, she could not stop thinking about Oliver. There had been no time to spend alone with him since he'd arrived. And she felt terrible about that. But he seemed to be taking it in his stride. One thing was for sure: the thing she'd feared the most, him getting along with her family and fitting in, had been all for naught. Her family liked him and he seemed to like them, as well. And he'd been so good with

Grandpa the previous night, so caring. It was a side of Oliver she was glad to have witnessed.

She was alone, as her mother was getting her manicure and Rachel was having her hair done. It was their last thing, and then they'd need to get home and get dressed before the photographer arrived.

As the technician buffed her feet and applied lotion, Annie couldn't help but wonder what would happen between her and Oliver once they returned to New York. Would they never see each other again? Would he ignore her if he ran into her in the elevator or the lobby? Somehow, she doubted that. Or at least she hoped not. Maybe they would meet up, for coffee or something? She didn't want to be too hopeful, but the last two days had gone incredibly well. Their disastrous blind date seemed like a lifetime ago.

"Look at us! All dolled up," Peggy said a short while later as they put on their coats.

"Thank you, Annie," Rachel said with tears in her eyes. She'd been weepy all morning.

Annie reached out and rubbed Rachel's shoulder. "No crying, Rach. You'll ruin your makeup."

The three of them held hands and grinned at each other.

"Stay here, I'll go get the car," Annie instructed. "We've got a wedding to get to!"

"We can walk," her mother protested.

"No, it's too cold and we don't want anything to happen to Rachel's hair," Annie said. Before they could say anything more, Annie went out the door to retrieve the car. As she walked along, she smiled. To think she'd been planning on not coming home for Christmas. She shook her head. She wouldn't have missed this for the world. How could she have been so foolish as to think otherwise?

The sun shone brightly, the snow a glittery landscape. It was going to be a beautiful day for a wedding.

Once home, they found Oliver and Malcolm together at the kitchen table, drinking coffee. Malcolm had a box of watches out and was showing Oliver various pieces. Oliver appeared interested and asked appropriate questions.

"Put that away, Malcolm," Peggy said. "Don't you know we have a wedding this afternoon? Are you ready?"

Malcolm pressed his lips together. "I've already showered. It will take me five minutes to put on my tux."

Peggy shook her head. Annie could tell her mother was beginning to get frazzled as every clock in the house ticked closer to the wedding.

"Mom, go up and get ready. I'll help Rachel," Annie said.

"Where's Grandma and Grandpa?" Peggy said. "They're not napping, are they?"

Malcolm closed the box. "Another time, Oliver."

"I look forward to it."

"You haven't answered my question about Grandma and Grandpa," Peggy said.

"They're dressed and ready to go. Oliver and I made them some sandwiches and tea, and they're watching television until it's time to leave." Malcolm stood up, placed his hands on Peggy's shoulders, and lowered his voice. "It's all right, love. We are going to have a wonderful day."

Peggy breathed an audible sigh of relief and hung on to her husband's arms. "You're right. Thank you." She placed her hand on the side of his face and smiled at him. "I'll go upstairs and get dressed." She turned to Annie and Rachel. "Go on, girls. I'll meet you in Rachel's room when I'm ready."

Dressed and ready, Annie left Grandma Fischer's room just as Oliver was coming out of her bedroom. He looked stunning in his navy suit and tie. Her breath caught in her throat and she thought, if only they were a real couple!

When he spotted her, he broke into a broad smile and walked toward her.

"Annie, you look beautiful!" he said. He spoke with such enthusiasm that Annie blushed. It mattered to her what he thought.

His cologne was swoon-worthy. And if he weren't staring at her, she'd close her eyes and take in a deep breath of it.

"Oliver, I want to thank you for being such a good sport these past few days," Annie said with a laugh. "Tomorrow's Christmas, and you're going to be stuck with me all day!"

He smiled. "I can't wait." His voice had such a rich timbre, and those eyes . . . She was excited about spending the whole day with him.

The door to Rachel's bedroom opened and she popped her head out, still dressed in her bathrobe. "Annie, are you coming?"

"Yes, of course," she said. She turned away from Oliver, but he had reached out and taken hold of her wrist. With a look of surprise on her face, she turned toward him. He raised her hand to his lips and kissed it.

"Thank you, Annie," he whispered. And with that, he bowed his head and headed downstairs, where everyone was waiting.

For a minute, she stood there, staring after him, holding her breath. Trying not to get excited and too full of hope.

Annie helped Rachel into her dress and began the process of fastening all the pearl buttons that ran down the back from the neck to the waist. Once she was finished, she took a step back and admired her sister.

"Rachel, I know it sounds like a cliché, but you are one beautiful bride," Annie said, her eyes brimming with tears.

Rachel turned toward her, and Annie set her veil on her head.

"I'm happy, Annie, I really am," Rachel said. "Brian is everything I ever hoped for."

Annie took both her sister's hands—she didn't want to hug her, for fear of wrinkling the dress. "Brian is wonderful, and I am so happy for you."

Rachel looked off to the side and then glanced back at Annie. "You know, Brad is wonderful too, in his own way."

Annie sighed. She didn't understand her sister's persistence on her getting back together with Brad. When she'd been with him, Rachel had never shown any interest. At all. Now, all of a sudden, it seemed as if it had become her life's mission to have them reconnect.

The last thing Annie wanted to do on Rachel's wedding day was to have words or end up arguing. She could have let it go, but instead she asked gently, "What's going on here? Why are you so determined to get me back with Brad?"

Rachel shrugged and looked away. It reminded Annie of when they were kids. Instead of just saying outright what bothered her, she remained coy.

Annie gently squeezed her sister's hands. "Come on, Rachel, why all the sudden interest in Brad and me?"

When Rachel looked at Annie, there were tears in her eyes. "I miss you, Annie. Ever since you moved to New York, I hardly ever see or even talk to you anymore."

Annie's chin quivered. She'd been so consumed with her own heartbreak she'd forgotten about those around her and how her move to the city had affected them.

"And what if you marry Oliver and the two of you decide to move to England? I'll never see you again!" Rachel's voice rose an octave.

"I am so sorry," Annie said, her voice shaking. Forgetting about the dress, she pulled her sister into a hug. "I will try to be a better sister. And you can call me or text me anytime you want."

When they pulled apart, Rachel looked down at the carpet. "I thought if you and Brad got back together, you'd come back to Hope Springs and we could go back to the way it was."

"Oh, Rachel," Annie said. "I don't need to get back together with Brad to be closer to you." Her mind raced as she thought of all the things they could do together going forward, all the things Annie was going to do to include Rachel in her life. "I'm going to work on this. I'm sorry. Please forgive me."

Rachel's expression softened. "You don't have to apologize, Annie. Everyone loves you. You're just so great."

Really? Now there were tears in Annie's eyes as she said, "And you're not so bad yourself."

There was a knock on the door and their mother entered. When she saw Rachel, her hands flew to her mouth. "Oh, Rachel!"

"I'll head downstairs," Annie said, thinking her mother and her sister might want to spend some time alone.

As Annie made her way down the staircase, she spotted Oliver standing with her father and her grandparents. He looked up at her and smiled. She was so getting used to that smile. She smiled back and for a bit, she indulged in the idea that he *was* her boyfriend. She knew that was dangerous thinking. But just for one day, that was all, she told herself. Because when he smiled at her, it was as if they were the only two people in the room.

A bright flash from the photographer's camera blinded her momentarily, and she reached out and held on to the banister to prevent herself from doing a tumble down the stairs.

Oliver stepped up and offered his hand as she descended.

"Annie, at the risk of sounding redundant, you look beautiful," he said truthfully.

She smiled broadly, and she stood on the tips of her toes and kissed him on his cheek. "Thank you, Oliver," she said. Realizing she'd left a red smudge of lipstick on his face, she laughed and wiped it off. She was aware that his eyes were on her, never leaving her face, and every nerve ending in her body tingled.

Grandma had tears in her eyes, and Grandpa dabbed his eyes with a handkerchief.

Malcolm glanced at his watch. "What's the holdup? Is she ready? We don't want to be late!"

Annie laid her hand on his arm. "It's all right, Dad. She's almost finished. She just wanted a few minutes alone with Mom."

"Well, I want a few minutes alone with her, too," he said.

"She'll be down in a minute," Annie soothed.

"My baby's getting married." He looked at Annie and then over to Oliver. "And next, it will be you." He sniffled and asked no one in particular, "Where has the time gone?"

At that moment, there was the sound of the opening and closing of a door upstairs, and Annie's mother descended the staircase. She was dressed in an emerald-green mother-of-the-bride outfit, and she was beaming. Malcolm opened his arms wide for his wife. "Peggy, you look as beautiful as the day I married you."

Rachel followed close behind her. Her gown was a confection of silk, lace, and satin. Annie thought she looked the part of a radiant bride, and she smiled to herself. She loved weddings. They were such happy affairs.

Mr. Beasley's eyes were full of tears as he stepped forward to offer his daughter his arm. "Rachel . . ." But he was unable to finish his sentence, as he started crying and had to pull out his handkerchief. Annie, Rachel, and their mother swarmed around him, comforting him.

Chapter Fourteen

As the newly married couple turned from the altar and were introduced as Mr. and Mrs. Hobart, the congregation clapped. Peggy had asked Oliver if he minded sitting with the grandparents, and he'd happily settled into a pew with Grandma Fischer and Grandpa Beasley. Right before the ceremony, Violet, who'd been seated behind them with Uncle Al and Aunt Betty, had slid into the pew with them, parking herself between Oliver and Grandma Fischer.

Oliver thought they were a lovely family. A little eccentric, but they all had such big hearts. And to think he would have spent Christmas alone in the city.

Throughout the ceremony, he'd been unable to take his eyes off of Annie. She was simply stunning. She'd been attentive of the bride and once, during the ceremony, she had giggled, and that had made Oliver smile. He watched her, mesmerized, thinking how glad he was that he'd gotten to know her better. He had almost missed out on all of this. He had almost missed out on getting to know the real Annie. Aware of eyes on him, he turned and noticed that Grandma Fischer was watching him. She smiled at him knowingly before turning her attention back to the altar.

The whole congregation stood as the newly married couple made their way down the center aisle, beaming. They were followed by the bridal party. Annie and Brad, as maid of honor and best man, were first to follow the couple. Oliver watched as Brad leaned in and whispered something, which resulted in a smile from Annie.

Oliver bit his lip and was confronted with a feeling he was unfamiliar with. Namely, jealously. Where had that come from? he wondered. The bridal party disappeared from the sanctuary and soon the pews began to empty, the guests gradually filing out. Uncle Al, Aunt Betty, and Violet hurried out the back to get to the Bristol Manor to oversee the dinner.

"Come on, time for the Bristol Manor," Grandma Fischer said. She eyed Oliver. "Annie told you to eat something beforehand, didn't she?"

Oliver nodded, unable to stop thinking of Annie and Brad walking arm in arm out of the church like they were next in line for matrimony.

"I love my daughter Betty, but she's a terrible cook," Grandma Fischer said, shaking her head.

Grandpa Beasley spoke up. "Who knows? Maybe we'll be surprised."

"Oh, we'll be surprised all right," Grandma said as she positioned her walker and got behind it. She and Grandpa Beasley were going out the back door to avoid the front steps. "Come on, Connie, I've got some meatloaf sandwiches in my purse."

"We'll see you at the Bristol Manor, Oliver," Grandpa Beasley said, following Grandma out.

Oliver nodded toward them and followed the rest of the crowd. When he arrived in the vestibule, he caught sight of Annie next to the groom, and on the other side of her was Brad, who was still talking in her ear. He decided to put an end to that once and for all.

After he congratulated the newlyweds, he approached Annie and said, "You look beautiful, darling," and before she could respond, he leaned down and kissed her on the lips. He could feel the surprise in her body, but her lips yielded to his. When he pulled back, she smiled tentatively, her face a mixture of confusion and surprise. He glanced at Brad, who simply stared at him. He extended his hand to Brad to shake. "Best man, is it?"

Mulled wine and hot appetizers were served at the Bristol Manor as the wedding party went off to take photographs. Oliver accepted a glass from a server, wondering what Annie was doing with Brad. Even the presence of Violet, stuck like glue at his side, couldn't distract him from those thoughts.

Grandma Fischer approached, pushing her walker ahead of her.

When she neared them, she said to Violet, "Your mother's calling you."

Violet smiled. "Okay, Grandma. Where is she?"

Grandma Fischer shrugged. "I don't know. Probably in the kitchen."

With a bounce and a skip in her step, Violet headed off to the kitchen.

Once Violet was out of earshot, Grandma said to Oliver, "I used to do that years ago with the neighborhood kids when my kids were younger. When they were getting on my nerves—which was all the time—I'd tell them their mother was calling them."

Oliver couldn't help but grin. "Even your own children?"

Grandma looked at him like he was stupid. "Not with my own kids." She paused and added, "I told them their father was looking for them."

Oliver laughed.

"I love Violet to pieces, but her obsession with the royal family gets to be a bit much. I blame Betty and Al for encouraging it by dragging her all over England." She looked thoughtful as she said, "Besides, you're here with Annie."

"I don't mind," Oliver said. "Violet is a lovely young lady."

"She is, that's for sure, but you need to spend more time with Annie," Grandma said.

The wedding party finally arrived, and Annie appeared flushed. Oliver hoped it was from the cold weather and not anything else.

"Speak of the devil," Grandma said.

As soon as Annie spotted Oliver, she left Brad's side and made her way over.

"This is my cue to exit," Grandma said, scurrying off as quickly as her walker would allow.

"I'm so sorry to keep you waiting," Annie said. "The place where Rachel wanted her pictures taken hadn't shoveled their walkways, so the groomsmen had to do that first." She laughed. She looked around and her eyes landed on the punch bowl in the middle of the reception table.

"Would you like some?" Oliver asked.

"Yes, please."

Oliver took the silver ladle and spooned punch into two glasses, handing one to Annie. He clinked his glass gently against hers. "To the prettiest bridesmaid I've ever seen."

An "oh" escaped her lips.

The urge to kiss her again was strong, and he gave that idea serious thought.

Annie's eyes followed a platter of appetizers going by. She looked at Oliver and asked, "How's the food so far?"

Oliver nodded. "What I've had has been delicious."

Annie's shoulders sagged in relief. "Oh, thank goodness. Rachel is so worried about the meal now."

"Annie, I must say again—" A dinner bell rang, and Oliver turned to look in the direction of the sound as it was announced that it was time to sit for dinner.

"Oliver, I've got to sit with the bridal party, but I'll join you as soon as the meal is finished," she said. "I'm so sorry. I didn't mean to leave you alone for such long periods of time."

Why did he feel like a pet when she put it like that? "Don't worry about it. I'm having a brilliant time," he said.

"You are?" she asked, doubt clouding her eyes.

"I am. Your grandparents are entertaining," he said. "And Violet has been keeping me company."

Annie laughed. She stepped up onto her tiptoes and kissed his cheek. "Thank you, Oliver, for being such a good sport. Thank you for everything."

He had no words, but reveled in her attention. More than anything, he would have liked to take her in his arms and kiss her properly, not caring who saw it.

And it wouldn't be for pretend.

The dinner choices were beef, salmon, or chicken. Oliver thought that overall, the food was very good. Even Grandma Fischer raved about it.

He kept his eye on the bridal party, more specifically Brad. He wanted to make sure Brad didn't get too close to Annie.

When the speeches had finished and the dancing had begun, Aunt Betty arrived at the table to enquire about the meal. Grandma Fischer said, "I don't have a clue what that starter was, it was all mashed together, but I have to admit that it was delicious. You should pat yourself on the back, Betty."

Everyone at the table concurred. Betty smiled sheepishly. "It's all down to our new assistant, Meg. She's a Culinary Institute graduate and she was looking for a job in Hope Springs. Luckily for us, there aren't many chef jobs here in town."

"My compliments to the chef," Grandpa Beasley said, waving his unlit cigar around. "Better hang on to her."

When Betty disappeared, Grandma Fischer took a drag off her electronic cigarette and observed, "Smartest decision Betty and Al ever made: hiring someone else to do the cooking. There's hope for them yet."

"Now, Oliver, tell me about this Phillipa person," Grandma Fischer directed. "And don't try to lie to me, because I can spot a liar within one hundred yards."

Oliver held his hands palms-up in mock surrender. "I've known Phillipa all my life. Our families are quite close. She's a good friend, but I think of her more like a sister than anything," he admitted.

Grandma narrowed her eyes at him. "And this Phillipa, does she view you like a brother?"

Oliver nodded. "Definitely. We're good friends. And on occasion, we're each other's default partner."

She continued to grill him. "Any chance it could turn into something more?"

Oliver shook his head. "No. She finds me repugnant."

Grandma looked taken aback. "Surely not."

"Surely yes," he said. "But she means it in a good way," he added quickly, not wanting to cast any aspersions on Phillipa. She'd been laughing when she said it all those years ago.

"There is a good way to be repugnant?" Grandma asked, skeptical.

"Apparently. She thinks I'm too stoic, too quiet, too dependable," Oliver explained, hardly believing he was having this conversation with Annie's grandmother.

"And are you?"

"I am," he said.

"Those are admirable traits," she pointed out. "What exactly is she looking for?"

"Someone a bit more bohemian," he said.

"This Phillipa sounds interesting," Grandma said, looking thoughtful.

Oliver gave a quick nod, thinking Grandma and Phillipa would get on well. He glanced around the room in search of Annie but saw her nowhere. He was going to ask her if she wanted to dance. He needed an excuse to take her in his arms. And the dancing was it.

"I'm a very old woman and I have one favor to ask you," Grandma said.

"Anything," Oliver said.

"Whatever happens between you and Annie, don't break her heart. I couldn't bear to watch that again," Grandma Fischer said softly. Suddenly the old woman, whom Oliver considered to be quite feisty, appeared frail.

"I promise," Oliver said.

"Good. I like you, Oliver, despite your title and money, and to be honest I don't like many people," Grandma said, her feistiness returning.

"Would you like to dance?" Oliver asked.

She burst out laughing. "You give me too much credit. But thank you for asking. I can't remember the last time someone asked me to dance," she said wistfully. "You've spent enough time with me. You should go find Annie."

He nodded and excused himself and looked around the reception room, but didn't see her. The bridal party had left the main table except for the bride and groom. They were leaning into each other, whispering and laughing as if they were the only two people in the room. Oliver thought them lucky.

As he exited the reception room, he spotted Annie in the atrium. His step faltered when he saw Brad with her.

His smile was replaced by a scowl as he watched Brad pull Annie into his arms. He stood there for a moment, dumbfounded.

How stupid had he been? The whole objective of Annie's arrangement was to make Brad jealous. And you'd only want to make a former boyfriend jealous if you still harbored feelings for him. Annie had still not noticed Oliver. Putting his hands in his pockets, he lifted his chin and headed back into the reception room. But as soon as he arrived, he changed his mind and decided that fresh air was in order. He turned and headed outside into the cold night.

Oliver hoped he didn't run into Annie's grandparents hanging out in the Cadillac, smoking. His mind was a flurry of emotions and there was something that he needed to think through. Something he needed to clear his head about.

The parking lot was crowded and the snow fell heavily. Oliver sighed and his breath came out in white wisps. He was sorry he didn't grab his coat on the way out; the air was bitter. He stamped his feet to stave off the cold. If he was going to do any thinking, he'd have to do it fast. His jealousy at seeing Annie with Brad had caught him on the back foot. Oliver reminded himself—again—that this was simply a mutual arrangement. But somewhere during the events of the previous days, something had shifted. And dared he say it? Oliver realized he was beginning to care for her. The feelings were there. The awful truth was he didn't want it to end.

But what to do about it? Could anything be done? How could he possibly compete with Brad if Annie was still in love with him?

Even though they'd gotten off on the wrong foot, he could see that Annie was someone special, and he'd be a fool not to pursue her. And this thought, so new and so confusing, unsettled him.

Say, on the outside chance, she was as interested as he was in pursuing a relationship. How would they deal with logistics? He didn't plan on remaining in New York forever. At some point, he would return to England. England was home. And he was pretty sure that Annie might someday want to return to Hope Springs. But he was getting ahead of himself. He wasn't even sure Annie felt about him the way he felt about her.

Finally, giving in to the cold, Oliver took hold of the brass door handle, pulled it open, and stepped inside. He didn't think he could feel any worse.

Chapter Fifteen

Annie searched everywhere for Oliver. She ended up in the atrium, wondering if he had wandered off for some quiet. She loved her family but to an outsider, they must seem overwhelming at times.

Her gaze traveled around the atrium, taking in the walls and ceilings made of glass and the white Christmas lights strung everywhere, including the lush palm trees and ferns. The furniture was Victorian white wicker and there was a glass-topped wicker table. In the corner was a white Christmas tree with red lights and ornaments. In the background, orchestral Christmas music played low.

It was magical. She wanted to find Oliver and show him this place.

"Annie!"

Brad. Annie's heart sank.

"There you are, I've been looking all over for you," Brad said.

"You found me," she said. As members of the wedding party, she and Brad had spent the majority of the day together. She felt she had more than put in her time with him. What she wanted now was to spend time with Oliver. Was that too much to ask?

"I was looking for Oliver." She hoped he might take the hint.

He didn't. "I wondered if you'd like to dance."

Annie frowned. Why would he ask her to dance? He knew she had a date for the wedding.

"No, I don't think so," she said. She lifted the hem of her gown to prevent her heel from getting caught and swept past him, but he reached out and took hold of her wrist.

"Hey, I'm getting the impression that you're avoiding me," he said.

"I'm not, Brad, it's just that I'm here with someone," she explained.

"I think we should talk," he said, letting go of her wrist.

"About what?" she asked. A feeling of dread filled her.

"About us."

Annie practically flinched. "Us? There is no us." Where had he been for the last year? Had he not noticed that she was no longer a part of his life?

"The biggest mistake I've ever made was breaking up with you," Brad said. He reached out and ran his finger along her forearm.

"Stop it," she warned, pulling her arm away. She crossed her arms in front of her.

"I thought I knew what I wanted. But when I made it to the top of Machu Picchu, all I could think about was you. It was such an incredible experience, one that was meant to be shared, and there I was, alone. You were the person I wished was there with me."

"And yet, it never occurred to you to call me or write to me?" Annie asked, flabbergasted. It just didn't make any sense.

Brad had the decency to look sheepish.

Annie put one hand on her hip, the other on her forehead, and gazed down at the floor for a minute before looking up. "Brad, I wanted to go with you on that trip. I begged you to take me with you. And you said no."

Brad exhaled a deep breath. "I regret that. I didn't know what I wanted then. I know now."

Annie scowled at him. "What are you talking about? Getting back together?"

"I'm asking for your forgiveness. I'm hoping we can start again."

"You do realize I have a date for this wedding," she said. Was he that thoughtless? Or clueless? Or both?

"I know, but that's a new relationship. Your mother told me you've only been going out for a few months."

Furious, Annie said, "You asked my mother about me?"

"Of course. Your mom always liked me," he said with a grin. "I bet she'd be happy if we got back together."

"You're incredible," Annie muttered.

"And you and I have history," he said. "Good history. And now that Brian has married Rachel, why not? It's the perfect way for us to get back together. What a story we can tell our grandchildren!"

"Wrap the whole thing up in a nice, neat bow," she said. The snark in her voice appeared to sail right past Brad.

"What do you say? Will we give it another try?" he asked.

"Let me see if I have this right," she said. She scratched her forehead and glanced at the floor. "You broke up with me because you wanted to go traveling. Alone. Now you're finished traveling, you're back in town, and you want to get back together?"

Brad had the decency to not say anything.

"Did you think I was just sitting around, waiting for you to return?" she asked. "I have a career and an apartment in New York. Am I to give all that up?"

It was Brad's turn to look down at the floor, his hands thrust in his pockets.

"When you went away, you left me no choice but to move on with my life. Without you," she said quietly. "Brad, I no longer feel the way I did about you."

He looked up at her. "I am sorry, Annie," he said sourly. "If I had just taken you with me . . ."

Annie reached over and placed her hand on his arm. "Sometimes, things work out the way they're supposed to."

He appeared to be struggling with something. There were deep lines in his forehead. Finally, he said, "It's my loss then."

Brad surprised her by throwing his arms around her and pulling her into a hug. Annie's eyes went wide and her body went rigid. As delicately as possible, she extricated herself from his embrace.

"Good luck to you, Brad," she said, stepping away from him and exiting the atrium.

Annie found Oliver standing with her father at the bar, deep in conversation. Now that the wedding was over, she was going to enjoy every moment with Oliver, her pretend boyfriend.

She tapped him on the shoulder and he turned to her. "Hello, there," she said.

His demeanor was inscrutable but his eyes were troubled. Annie frowned and he broke eye contact.

"Annie!" her father said.

"Hi, Dad," she said. "Enjoying yourself?"

"Am I? This has been the best Christmas ever," he said, pulling her into a hug and kissing her on the forehead. Her father was rarely this exuberant or openly affectionate. The wedding had made him both nostalgic and demonstrative.

"I'm going to mingle," he announced.

Her father walked off and the first person he came across, he threw up his arms and greeted them with a hug. She laughed.

"Oh boy, Dad's having a great time," she said. She turned back to Oliver. She wanted to ask Oliver to dance but he was acting strangely, so she didn't. A part of her hoped he would ask her, instead.

He stood next her, barely saying a word.

Annie didn't know what to say. Had something happened? Had someone insulted him? Had she done something to offend him? She rubbed the back of her neck absentmindedly and watched the couples dancing on the dance floor.

Violet approached them, and Annie thought how pretty she looked in her dress with the full skirt and the red satin sash around her waist. Annie was relieved for the interruption as the silence between her and Oliver had grown uncomfortable.

"Oliver," Violet started. She glanced at Annie, then back to Oliver, and smiled shyly. "Would you like to dance with me?"

Oliver set his empty glass on the bar and smiled. "I would love to."

Annie bit her lip, trying not to feel hurt. She couldn't understand the change that had come over him. What had happened?

At midnight, a coffee-and-tea station was set up by the staff of the Bristol Manor. Annie helped her mother, Aunt Betty, and the rest of her aunts set out the platters of Christmas cookies and dessert bars. In the run-up to the wedding, the ovens of every baker in the extended family had been running at full throttle. Plates and platters of delectable Christmas treats covered the length of the trestle table. Annie's mother directed everything. How the mint bars, which were green, would look best next to the cranberry-oatmeal cookies. Annie laughed as her mother snuck a cookie and shoved it into her mouth.

They all stood back and admired their handiwork.

"Betty, these eggnog cookies are to die for!" Peggy said, enthusiastically helping herself to another.

"Meg! It's all Meg," Aunt Betty gushed.

Annie was proud of her mother. Christmas had always been a big holiday in the Beasley household but this year, in addition to the holiday, her mother had managed to organize, delegate, and put together an amazing wedding on a shoestring budget.

Annie hugged her mother, who looked surprised. "Mom, you've done a fabulous job. If no one else has thanked you for it yet, I want to be the first."

Peggy patted Annie's shoulder. "I enjoyed every minute of it." She continued, "Boy, that Oliver is a keeper. Dancing with your cousin like that. I think our Violet has a little bit of a crush on him."

Annie swallowed hard and looked around the ballroom, narrowing her eyes to get a better focus. "He is, isn't he?" She couldn't help but remember the fun they'd had at his Christmas party, when they had danced all night. She had loved being in his arms and had hoped to be in his arms again tonight.

"Promise me that if you two should ever get married, you'll do it here in Hope Springs. I couldn't bear not to have a hand in my daughter's wedding."

Annie's face turned beet red. "Mom, we've only been seeing each other for a few months," Annie stammered. "Who knows if it will last?"

Peggy made a dismissive gesture with her hand. "Annie, you mustn't think like that just because of one bad experience."

One bad experience that had changed her whole life. And now this one, even though it was fake, was heading in the same direction at apparent breakneck speed.

"Your father and I like Oliver. Despite his station in life, he's down-to-earth. You'd think those types would be snobs, wouldn't you? But he isn't."

"No, he isn't, is he?" Annie agreed.

"Anyway, he's a good man and he's good for you—I feel it in my waters," Peggy said.

"Oh, Mom!"

A line began to form at the dessert table. Oliver approached her.

Her heart skipped a beat at the sight of him. Maybe it was the wedding. Maybe it was Christmas, or maybe it was the combination of the two, but she smiled at the sight of him. He certainly was the whole package, and the bonus was that accent.

For a moment, awkwardness ensued and this bothered Annie. She had thought they'd fallen into an easy, companionable place. But that seemed to have disappeared and she didn't know why.

"There are coffee and tea and some desserts," she said, searching his face. What had happened? He appeared so—*resigned*?

"Are you all right?" she asked. She laughed nervously and said, "You look like you just lost your best friend."

He didn't smile. "I'm going to see if I can get a flight back to the city in the morning."

Annie's mouth opened slightly and she blinked. "On Christmas Day?" she asked. Disappointment crushed her. "Why?"

"The wedding's over and our arrangement has come to an end," he said.

Annie's neck felt hot and her voice shook. "I suppose it has."

She had been right. It was strictly business. And he had been a great actor. They had been getting along so well these past few days, but now he was showing a side of himself that reminded her of the person she had met back in October. Haughty and arrogant.

Well, fine. If he wanted to go back to the city that was his prerogative, but he could at least explain what had gone wrong.

He started to walk away from her and Annie reached out for him.

"Oliver, please tell me what's wrong," she said. "What has happened that you want to fly out on Christmas morning and be alone in the city for the holiday? I mean, I know my family is a bit eccentric, and I know it's not the same as being with your own family, but still, the holidays are meant to be shared."

"Ahh . . ."

"Am I really that bad? Is my family that awful? You seemed to be getting on well with them."

"Oh no, your family is great," Oliver said hurriedly. "In a short period of time, I've grown very fond of them."

Annie stood in front of him and said plainly, "Then it's me." She looked around, unable to make eye contact with him. "I thought things were going well between us. Better than I even expected."

Oliver drew in a breath and exhaled loudly. "Annie, I feel like I'm in the way."

Annie frowned and repeated, "In the way? In the way of what?"

Oliver looked down at the ground. Then looked up at her. "Once I'm gone, the way is clear for you and Brad to get back together."

"What? Why would you say something like that?"

"Two things, actually," Oliver said. "Brad told me he wants you back. He said, and I quote, 'I intend to win Annie back.' And then, I saw the two of you together in the atrium—"

"Yes, he came up to me in the atrium and asked me to get back together with him, which I point-blank refused." Annie fumed. She pressed her lips together, gathering her thoughts. "I can't control what comes out of Brad's mouth. But I'm not getting back together with him. I don't want to get back together with him. Maybe you could give me a little credit."

Oliver ran his hand through his hair and looked around.

She fixed her gaze on everyone standing in line for coffee and desserts.

Oliver shifted on his feet and said with a small laugh, "I will say I'm relieved to hear that." He paused and looked at her. "I've made a right bollocks of things, haven't I?"

Annie deflated. "Whatever that is, then yes you have. You assumed something that was grossly mistaken and exaggerated," she said. "And what's more, you ruined a perfectly good evening. We could have had a great time together."

"I'm sorry," Oliver said. "For drawing the wrong conclusions. I should have asked."

"Why didn't you?" she asked.

He shrugged. "I don't know." Finally, he admitted, "Probably because I was afraid of the answer."

Annie didn't say anything.

"Forgive me," he said quietly, looking at her.

"It's all right, Oliver, it was just mixed signals," Annie said, her voice tired. She turned around and walked away.

In two strides, Oliver was at her side. He took hold of her hand. Surprised, she looked up at him.

"Annie, please stay with me," Oliver said softly.

Annie smiled and leaned closer to him.

The bandleader announced, "This will be the last song of the evening."

"Will you dance this last dance with me?" Oliver asked.

Annie bit her lip as her heart thrummed. "I would love to."

As the evening drew to a close, the snow was piling up outside. The wedding guests started bundling up and saying their goodbyes. Rachel and Brian headed off to their bridal suite at the hotel.

The Beasleys were the last ones to leave the Bristol Manor. By now it was three in the morning. Annie drove her parents and Oliver in her car. Her grandparents had been driven home earlier, before the snow had started falling. Annie inched her way home. Her fatigue was quickly replaced with anxiety as she leaned forward in the driver's seat, maintaining a white-knuckled grip on the steering wheel.

"I've never seen this much snow," Oliver said quietly.

"Don't you get snow in England?" she asked. She was so glad he was talking. A glance in the rearview mirror showed her mother with her head on her father's shoulder, sound asleep. Her father had his eyes closed, too.

"We do, but not like this," he said. And then he fell silent.

She quickly looked over at him, his face illuminated by the dashboard lights. If she wasn't so nervous about driving, she'd sigh. He had some real swoony looks going on over there.

Annie pulled into the driveway. There had to be three feet of snow. Gently, she woke her parents to let them know they were home.

They got out of the car, and Annie groaned as the snow went up to her knees. She wore high-heeled shoes, and she shivered in the little faux-fur stole she wore over her bridesmaid dress. Oliver rounded the car toward her, removing his overcoat, and put it over her shoulders before she could protest.

"Take my arm so you don't slip," Oliver said.

Ahead of them, Malcolm and Peggy hung on to each other as they navigated the driveway and made their way to the back door.

They stepped across the threshold, and Annie let out the breath she'd been holding. She didn't want to remove Oliver's coat. It was heavy and warm and most of all, it smelled of his aftershave. She wondered if he'd mind if she slept in it.

"Oh, look at the state of us," Peggy said. "Will I make some coffee?"

Malcolm declined, yawning. "It's been a long day. I'm going to bed."

"Annie? Oliver?"

"Mom, if you're tired, go on up to bed. I can make something for Oliver and me," Annie said.

"Do you mind? It has been such a long day. A great day, but a long one," Peggy said.

"It was a great day," Annie agreed. And it had been. "Will I bring you up a cup of tea?"

Peggy smiled at her daughter. "That's thoughtful, but by the time the kettle boils, I'll be sound asleep. I'll see you both in the morning. Sleep in, because no one is going anywhere in the morning." She smiled. "Merry Christmas to both of you."

"Happy Christmas, Mrs. Beasley," Oliver said.

Once they were alone, Annie turned to him. "Would you like cocoa or maybe tea?"

"I'm tired as well, and think I might just head to bed," Oliver said, yawning.

"Oh, okay." Annie removed his coat and handed it to him. "Thank you."

They walked up the staircase together and stopped outside Annie's bedroom.

Oliver turned to look at her. "Annie, thank you for inviting me here. I'm having a wonderful time."

"I'm so glad to hear that, Oliver," Annie said. There was a slight pause before she admitted, "I'm happy you're here."

They regarded each other, and Oliver leaned in. Annie had just reached up to touch the side of his face when the door to Grandma Fischer's bedroom opened. She saw them, smiled, and winked. "Pay no attention to me. I'm just an old woman in need of the bathroom."

Annie stepped back and cleared her throat. "Good night, Oliver."

Annie had her flannel pajamas on by the time Grandma Fischer returned from the bathroom.

"Do you need any help, Grandma?" Annie asked.

"No, Annie, I'm fine," she said, and she backed up until her calves hit the edge of the bed. She left her walker next to the bed, sat down, and slowly swung her legs up and underneath the blankets. Annie smoothed the covers out over her grandmother.

Annie went to the bathroom, washed her face, and brushed her teeth. Within five minutes, she was climbing into the bed next to her grandmother.

Grandma turned off the bedside light, and the dark room glowed with alternating beams of red and green light from outside.

"Oh, I forgot to turn the floodlights off," Annie said with a groan. She flipped the covers back, but Grandma laid her hand on her arm.

"Leave it. It's kind of nice, the different-colored lights," she said. "And it is Christmas, so just this once it will be all right. Merry Christmas, Annie."

"Merry Christmas, Grandma," Annie said, and she leaned over and kissed her on the cheek. Her grandmother smelled of Nina Ricci and the rose-milk lotion she used on her face every night.

The two of them settled down. This wasn't the first time Annie had to bunk with her grandmother. Any time there was a houseful of people, Annie's room was the first to go. Rachel had bunked once with Grandma Fischer but it turned out she was a restless sleeper, and Grandma woke up the following morning with bruises on her shins and thus declared her bed a Rachel-free zone.

"I like that Oliver of yours very much," Grandma said.

Annie rolled over onto her side so that she faced her grandmother. "I like him, too."

"He's so well suited to you."

"I think so too," Annie said.

"Much better than that Brad," Grandma said with a sigh.

"You didn't like him, did you?"

"No, because he was selfish," Grandma replied. "He started every sentence with 'I.' When you're part of a couple, you should start every sentence with 'We.'"

Annie stared out the window and made a note of that.

CHAPTER SIXTEEN

Sunshine streamed through the windows of Annie's bedroom, waking Oliver. He opened his eyes, blinked, sat up, and peered out the window at all the snow. Then he remembered it was Christmas morning. His wristwatch hung off the bedpost and he glanced at it; it was almost ten. He didn't get up right away, choosing to remain in bed.

He hadn't meant to be rude to Annie the previous night and deep down, he had to admit that his behavior had been shameful. He sighed. Normally, he wasn't the jealous type, but there was something about Brad that pressed his buttons. And to be jealous over a girlfriend who wasn't even his? He had lost the plot. Yet she had forgiven him. Not that he deserved it. The one dance they had had at the end of the evening had made up for it.

It was the look on Annie's face when he'd told her that he was thinking of flying out early that had affected him the most. *Crushed* would be how he would describe it. He had hurt her. He groaned inwardly at the thought of it.

Nothing gave him the right to treat her poorly. He was better than that. And Annie didn't deserve it. He remembered his promise to her grandmother. Despite the late hour when he went to bed, he'd lain awake for a long time, thinking of the future and all the possibilities with Annie.

When he began to hear voices and movement downstairs, Oliver got up and showered, dressed, and headed downstairs.

Annie, her parents, and grandparents were in the living room, exchanging gifts.

"Happy Christmas," Oliver said, feeling as if he were intruding on a private family moment.

They all wished him a Merry Christmas, and he handed Annie, Peggy, and Grandma Fischer wrapped gifts before taking a seat on the sofa next to Annie.

All three women were delighted, and Oliver shrugged sheepishly. "It's just a little something for your hospitality."

He watched as Annie opened her gift, a red silk scarf. Red was her color.

"Oh, Oliver, it's beautiful!" she said and then looked at him, her face falling with embarrassment. "I'm sorry, I didn't get you anything."

He smiled at her to reassure her. "Don't worry about it." She had given him a lot of fun and somewhere to go at Christmas. And that was better than any gift.

"Oliver, thank you for the gloves," Peggy said. She looked at her husband and whispered, "They're real leather, and they're lined with faux fur." They both raised their eyebrows.

Peggy stood up, retrieved a gift from beneath the tree, and handed it to Oliver. "Merry Christmas, Oliver."

Oliver was touched. Annie's mother had been so busy and yet she had managed to get him something for Christmas. He opened it up to find a pair of Christmas pajama pants with a solid-color thermal top. Thankfully, the pants were relatively understated: navy with white snowflakes. "Thank you."

They sat there for a bit longer, going over their gifts, and Peggy yawned. "It's almost noon. We should eat breakfast. And then you're on your own."

Annie laughed. "All right, Mom."

Oliver looked from Annie to her mother and back again.

"When the girls were little, I'd be so exhausted by the time Christmas morning rolled around, I'd have to take a nap in the afternoon. That's become a tradition,"

Peggy explained. "Now, after brunch, Malcolm and I take a nap. We'll have dinner at six."

If anyone deserved a nap, it was Peggy Beasley, Oliver thought.

They spent Christmas brunch at the kitchen table, eating and drinking and going over all the events of the day before. There were blueberry pancakes, a scrambled-egg strata, mimosas, and bacon and sausage. Rachel and Brian were absent, opting to spend the day with his family.

Annie hadn't said much to Oliver all morning, and he was anxious to be alone with her.

"Mom, we can do the cleanup. You and Dad go on upstairs and we'll take care of everything," Annie said.

Peggy looked around at all the dirty dishes on the table and the pans on the stovetop. "Are you sure?"

"I'll help," Oliver chimed in.

Peggy hesitated. "All right then. Come on, Malcolm, time for our Christmas afternoon nap."

Grandma Fischer and Grandpa Beasley headed to the living room to watch television. They were excited about Christmas Day programming.

Oliver cleared the table as Annie loaded the dishwasher. Once it was full, she put soap in it, closed it, and turned it on. There were two pans she washed by hand and gave to Oliver to dry.

"Where will I put the dish towel?" Oliver asked.

Annie nodded toward the AGA. "Just hang them on the towel rack overhead." As he did that, she threw more wood into the range.

"Will we go for a walk and get some fresh air?" Annie asked when they were finished.

Once out the door, he squinted against the bright afternoon sun. It was cold and the snow crunched beneath his boots. She walked at his side. She looked tired, he thought. Yesterday had been a day full of excitement, and it had been a late night.

"Oliver, I can't thank you enough," Annie started. "You've been the perfect boyfriend."

He smiled. If she only knew how he felt about her. He'd rather be her *real* boyfriend. "It was easy," he said. "And I've had a lot of fun. Your family are crackers but in a good way."

Annie laughed. "Yes, they are."

They walked along the road for a while, quiet.

Finally, Annie said, "We have one more day here tomorrow, and I thought we'd go into town."

"Sounds good," he said.

There was so much he wanted to say, but something held him back. They walked a little more until they gave in to the cold weather and turned around and headed back. When they arrived at the house, Oliver said, "Look, Annie, I know you're wrecked, so if you want to rest, I don't mind. I can amuse myself."

Annie laughed, her eyes bright and merry. "Don't be silly, Oliver. Just because everyone in my family seems to favor napping, doesn't mean I do. How old do you think I am?"

Oliver grinned. He wondered if she knew how lovely she was. "I just don't want you to feel obligated to entertain me."

She punched him playfully on his arm. "I'm not obligated to do anything. I want to hang out with you this afternoon."

Oliver was all for that.

But her smile disappeared and her voice faltered, "Unless of course, *you* want to take a nap."

He shook his head. "No, I do not. Hanging out, as you said, sounds good to me."

"What would you like to do? We could watch a movie or play some board games?"

"Either, I don't mind, you decide," he said.

Peggy, Malcolm, Grandma Fischer, and Grandpa Beasley went up to bed early Christmas night, all four citing exhaustion from the wedding and the holiday. That left Annie alone with Oliver.

The two of them had spent the afternoon at the dining room table, playing board games and eating Christmas cookies until it was time to help with dinner. Right before they all sat down, Oliver rang his parents and wished them a Happy Christmas.

At the end of the night, Oliver had to admit to being tired. But he loved every minute of being with Annie, and he didn't want it to end. Any of it.

Annie poured two glasses of eggnog and asked Oliver to open the tin of caramel crunch. On the cover was a winter scene of a sleigh being pulled by two horses. It made Oliver nostalgic for home and Christmases past.

They set the eggnog and the caramel crunch down on the coffee table in the living room. Annie turned on the electric fireplace to give the room atmosphere. There was no need to switch on any of the table lamps, as there were Christmas lights strung around the tree, along the mantel, and lining the windows. Annie put the CD player on low and joined him on the sofa.

She leaned forward, reaching for the eggnogs, and handed one to Oliver.

He clinked his glass mug with hers. "Happy Christmas, Annie."

"Merry Christmas, Oliver."

They were quiet, each staring at the fire. Then Oliver looked down at his eggnog as he sipped it. "I want to thank you for the lovely Christmas. I was unable to go home and to me, Christmas is such a family holiday that I wasn't looking forward to spending it alone in the city."

Annie gestured toward the ceiling, glass in hand. "Then thank goodness my mother invited you."

"Yes, thank goodness for that, or I'd be in Manhattan on my own," he said with an expression of distaste on his face. "I'd hate that." He lifted his glass toward the ceiling in a toast to Peggy.

Annie took a handful of caramel crunch.

"And what about you, Annie? I had the impression that you didn't want me to stay."

Annie shifted in her seat. "Um . . ." she started.

"That's doesn't sound promising," Oliver teased.

"No, honestly, I would have liked you to stay, but I wouldn't have wanted you to feel obligated," she said. "Mostly I was nervous about us being together all the time."

Oliver frowned and helped himself to some of the candy. "Why would you think that?"

Annie shrugged. "Because our arrangement was strictly business. We hardly knew each other." Annie swallowed some eggnog.

"It may have started out like that, but I think we've spent enough time together over the last three days to perhaps . . . we've moved outside the realm of an arrangement and into—dare I say it? A friendship?"

Annie nodded. "I think so."

They were quiet, each lost in their thoughts.

"I could use a friend in the city," she admitted. "I haven't formed any new friendships other than Carol and Doug."

"I'm the same way," he said, leaning forward and resting his elbows on his knees. "When you're working all the time, it's hard to find the motivation for anything extra."

Annie listened, eating pieces of caramel crunch from her hand.

"When I moved to New York, I had all these plans," he said. "Visit the Statue of Liberty, go out for breakfast on a Sunday morning, run in Central Park, go to a Broadway show. I've been there for a year and aside from running in Central Park, I've done none of that. Now, I'm not afraid to do those things by myself, but it would be nice to have some company . . ." He left his sentence hanging.

Annie didn't say anything.

Oliver looked shyly at her. "When we get back to the city, would you maybe be interested in meeting up and doing some of those things together?" he asked. He tilted his head.

"Sure," she said. "I'd love to."

"Great, I'll look forward to it," he said with an earnest smile.

"Me, too," she agreed readily.

Oliver set his empty glass on the table. He didn't think he could eat or drink one more thing. They spoke of all the things in New York City each of them would like to do and made a promise to meet up once they returned. Although he would have loved if it was more than friendship she was offering, he'd settle for friendship only. And who knew? Maybe it would blossom into something else. He was hopeful. Suddenly, he was anxious to get back and get started on this new chapter of their relationship.

At the end of the night, Annie and Oliver carried their dishes back into the kitchen.

"That's a great range," Oliver said, nodding toward the AGA.

"That's Aggie," she said. As if she'd been cued, she filled a kettle, set it on top of the stove, and closed the damper.

"You named your stove?" Oliver said with a laugh.

"She's been Aggie for as long as I can remember," Annie said. "I can't imagine the kitchen without her. Especially on those cold winter mornings."

"We have one at our home, too," Oliver said.

"Once when I was a kid, I was standing in front of it, all ready to go to school, and when I walked away the whole back of my coat was gone."

Oliver looked at her in surprise. "Were you hurt?"

Annie shook her head. "No, I didn't even realize it at the time. The synthetic material on the outside of the coat melted, but the cotton filling was still there. We still laugh about it to this day."

Oliver leaned against the sink and Annie joined him. A curl had escaped her ponytail and absentmindedly, Oliver reached out and tucked it behind her ear. His gaze landed on the mistletoe hanging above their heads. He frowned in confusion.

"Why is there mistletoe hanging over the kitchen sink?" he asked. It was certainly unorthodox, but nothing would surprise him anymore in this household. It was one of the many reasons he'd grown so fond of this family so quickly.

Annie laughed. "My mother put it there. She spends so much time in the kitchen that it reminds her and Dad that they need to kiss each other every once in a while."

"I like that idea," he said. He glanced at the mistletoe and then back at Annie, hesitating. Annie watched him with interest.

He inched closer to her and lowered his voice. "I know it's a cliché, but it is Christmas."

Annie nodded with a smile, and that gave Oliver all the encouragement he needed. It was as if it happened in slow motion. He laid his hand gently on the side of her face and Annie closed her eyes. He began to lean toward her but stopped, and Annie opened her eyes to see what was happening.

Oliver grinned. "Annie Beasley, if I'm going to kiss you, I'm going to kiss you properly."

Annie bit her lip and smiled.

He took her in his arms and pulled her close to him. She felt so good—better than he'd imagined. All soft and curvy. The thing he'd been wanting to do for a long time, he did: he kissed her, liking how her lips molded against his, liking how she kissed him back, reveling in it. They stood beneath the mistletoe at the kitchen sink, and he kissed her good and long.

The kitchen door opened, startling Oliver and Annie out of their embrace. Both were flushed and breathless.

"Oh, I'm so sorry," Peggy said with a grin. "Your father is having indigestion and I came down for the antacid."

She opened a cupboard, grabbed the bottle, and exited the room. As she did, she waved and said, "As you were!"

Oliver and Annie burst out laughing.

By midnight, as they walked up the stairs, Oliver felt encouraged by the sudden turn of events.

As they reached the first landing, the grandfather clock gonged midnight and Oliver jumped. Annie covered her mouth to suppress her giggles.

Oliver laughed and whispered, "I don't think I'll ever get used to that. I feel like I'm away at boarding school and I've got to run down to the main dining room for my bowl of watery porridge and a heel of bread."

Annie leaned against the wall, laughing, holding her stomach.

"I'm sorry. My father likes clocks," she said.

"You don't say!" Oliver said in mock surprise.

They stood outside Annie's old room. He had his hand on the doorknob. He smiled at her and Annie warmed on the inside.

"What would you have done in the city for Christmas?" she asked.

He shrugged. "I don't know. I'm sure there would be things open. Go to a church service in the morning. Walk around Manhattan. I was even considering cooking a turkey."

"Really?" she asked, impressed.

"Although I'm not the best cook—actually, I know little—it just seemed like the thing to do. I wouldn't have wanted to go out for dinner; to me, it seems depressing to eat out on a holiday."

There was silence before he said, "You would have come home for Christmas? To Hope Springs?"

"I had been thinking of spending Christmas in New York this year," Annie admitted.

"Really? Why?" he asked.

"Just something different," she said. "But then Rachel decided to get married at Christmas and that changed my plans."

"And here we are," Oliver said. Then quietly, he added, "Although, in an alternate universe, if we had both ended up in the city at Christmas, maybe we could have done something . . . together."

"Like, you cook the turkey and I'll bring the spuds and the veg?"

Oliver laughed. "Yes, something very much like that."

The thought of the two of them alone for Christmas, cooking dinner together, filled Oliver with all sorts of wonderful ideas.

Annie lingered and he kissed her again. He didn't want to go to bed. He would have stayed up all night with her.

Chapter Seventeen

The day after Christmas, Annie and Oliver strolled down Main Street in Hope Springs, her arm looped through his at his insistence. Oliver said they might as well keep up the pretense, in case they ran into anyone from the wedding.

Annie was more than happy to go along with that idea. She could certainly get used to the idea of Oliver being her boyfriend. She hadn't felt this happy in a long time. She was excited to return to the city, knowing that she would be seeing him again. She was thinking of starting slow, maybe inviting him for breakfast or to go walking in Central Park. That thought evolved into a fantasy of a romantic carriage ride around the park. When he'd admitted he'd hardly made any friends in New York because he'd worked so much, she'd felt as if she'd found a kindred spirit.

But it was more than that. Annie felt ready to step out of her comfort zone. She'd been in New York for a year and aside from going to work, she'd rarely stepped out of her apartment. Now, with Oliver, she was ready to explore the city and all it had to offer.

Oliver stopped in front of Perk Avenue, a coffee shop that also offered homemade baked goods.

"Will we get some coffee and something to eat?" he asked, peering inside.

Annie nodded and smiled. "Sounds like a good idea."

As they opened the door to the shop, Oliver's cell phone rang. He retrieved it from his pocket and frowned. "It's Mr. Hardcastle. Excuse me, Annie, but I'd better take this."

"No problem. I'll go in and grab us a table."

"Great, be with you in a moment," he said, and he swiped the screen on his phone and answered hello.

Annie slipped inside, reveling in the warmth and the smell of fresh-brewed coffee. She snagged a table by the window and was able to watch Oliver on the sidewalk outside.

He stood in profile to her, his expression one of full concentration. He broke into a wide grin and started speaking. Annie couldn't hear what was being said, but it appeared to be good news. Hopefully, he'd gotten the promotion he wanted.

When he finished the phone call, he gave a small nod and turned around. When he spied her, he grinned and gave her the thumbs-up. He strode through the coffee shop until he reached their table.

Annie was dying to know the content of the conversation but she didn't want to appear nosy. Instead, she suggested they go up to the counter and put in their orders for coffee and a pastry.

Once they ordered—peppermint mocha and a glazed donut for Annie and tea and a muffin for Oliver—they were told by the waitress that she'd bring their order over to them. Annie took the little tabletop stand that had the number four on it and carried it back to their table. She was in a great mood, and now it seemed there was going to be something to celebrate.

The server brought over their order, and Oliver grinned as they stirred their hot beverages.

Annie leaned forward, elbows on the table, her mocha between her hands. "I think you might have some good news."

"I do." Oliver beamed. "And you're the first person I want to share it with."

She was dying to ask if he'd got his promotion but she didn't want to steal his thunder.

Oliver squeezed a bit of lemon into his tea. "That was Mr. Hardcastle. He's offered me a promotion."

Annie set her mocha down and reached over and squeezed Oliver's arm. "Oh, Oliver, congratulations! I'm so happy for you."

"I can't believe it," he said, grinning, looking out the window.

"So, you got a promotion?" she asked, taking a bite of her donut.

"Better than what I expected," Oliver said.

Annie waited for him to explain.

"Mr. Hardcastle is opening up a branch in London and he wants me to run it! I just couldn't believe it! I never expected anything like that! And Annie, I owe it all to you. He asked after you, by the way," Oliver said.

Annie's shoulders slumped slightly. His good news was her bad news. He'd be returning to England with his coveted promotion and she'd never see him again. The budding friendship that they'd talked about the previous night wouldn't even get off the ground. There'd be no meetups on Saturdays or workday lunches. There'd be no walks through Central Park or Broadway shows. All her hopes were dashed at that moment. A part of her had believed their friendship might lead to something more. But she could see now that that thought hadn't even occurred to him. From the beginning, they had not been on the same page. *I'm a fool,* she thought bitterly.

She plastered a smile on her face. No matter how she felt, she would not ruin his happiness. And most of all, she'd make sure he never knew how she really felt about him.

Oliver focused on his muffin, cutting it into precise quarters with his knife, all the while talking about his plans and good fortune. He was still speaking as he spread butter on his muffin. He stopped, set his knife down, and looked at Annie.

"I'm sorry, Annie. I must sound incredibly dull," he said. His smile was gone and his expression was full of concern.

Annie shook her head. "Not at all! I want to hear all about it! I'm so happy for you." Wasn't that how you were supposed to feel for your friend? Supportive? Enthusiastic? But she had wanted so much more than friendship.

"Although I had hoped to stay in New York for another year or two, this is too good an opportunity to pass up," he said.

"It is," Annie said. "And you can visit New York anytime."

"I'm sure I'll be back for business, at least," he said.

"I'm sure." She tried to smile encouragingly. It must have worked, because he was still talking.

An uplifting Christmas song played in the background. It was the type of song that made you want to join in and sing along. But Annie felt far from joining in. She was acutely aware of a small seed of sadness taking root inside her.

"Do you know when you'll be returning to England?" she asked. Why did she feel like crying?

Oliver swallowed a bite of his muffin and wiped his mouth with a napkin. "Mr. Hardcastle didn't say definitively. He said we'll discuss it in January."

That was next month. Most likely, Mr. Hardcastle would want to get Oliver back to England as soon as possible.

Annie felt sad, as if an opportunity was whistling right past her. All the Christmas music playing and the decorations made her both nostalgic and sad.

"Before I leave, I'd like to take you to dinner," Oliver said.

"That isn't necessary," Annie said. *England gets her son back and I get a dinner.* She inhaled deeply and held her breath.

"After all, this is your success as much as it is mine."

Annie highly doubted that. All she'd done was show up as his girlfriend for his Christmas party. It wasn't she who had done all the hard work during the past year. And she knew Oliver's work ethic was similar to her own.

Oliver admired the view outside the window. "This is a great little town. Reminds me of home in a way."

"It is," Annie agreed, looking around at the shops lining Main Street. Something tugged at her heart.

"It seems we have the whole day to do anything we want," Oliver observed. "What would you like to do, Annie?"

Annie pressed her lips together. What would she like to do? Honestly, she'd like to place her hands on either side of his face and kiss him. Kiss him well, so he wouldn't forget her.

"Um, Annie? Hello?" Oliver asked.

She spotted the old cinema with its red-and-gold marquee across the street. "Oh, look, *It's a Wonderful Life* is playing at the old movie house. I'd love to see that," she said. She could sit there in the dark for two hours and not have to think about him moving back to England. And she wouldn't have to hold up her end of the conversation. She didn't think she could do it. The thought of it exhausted her.

"You know, I'm ashamed to admit I've never seen that film."

Annie raised an eyebrow. "Really? Then that settles it. Because it's a classic."

It was late afternoon and almost dark by the time they emerged from the cinema. Snow was falling lightly.

Oliver was animated as they walked along the sidewalk toward Annie's car.

"That was a great movie. I can't believe I've never seen it before," Oliver said. He glanced over his shoulder at the old movie house. "It's amazing that your cinema has lasted all these years. It feels almost nostalgic, doesn't it?"

Annie nodded. "It does."

"Here, Annie, you'd better take my arm, the footpath is icy," Oliver said.

Annie looped her arm through his, and it felt like a natural thing to do. "When I was a kid, my mother took me to see *The Sound of Music*. She felt that the television didn't do justice to certain movies and they needed to be viewed on the big screen."

"Now, I have seen that one. An awful lot of singing in that movie," Oliver said.

Annie laughed. "Yes, there was."

"I prefer old black-and-white movies," Oliver said. "I used to watch them with my grandmother."

"Did you?" Annie asked. She tried to picture him as a young boy.

"Her favorite was *Mrs. Miniver*, so we watched that one a lot," he said.

"That's a great movie, too."

They reached the car and found it covered in snow. Several inches must have fallen while they were in the cinema.

"Annie, why don't you get in and start the car and I'll brush it off?" Oliver suggested.

"I'll help."

Oliver put up his hand. "No, I insist. I'll have it done in no time."

Annie slid into the driver's seat, turned on the car, and shivered. It had been a pleasant day. As Oliver brushed off the car, Annie watched him, getting lost in a reverie of the two of them sitting around watching old black-and-white movies. It was painfully pleasant.

But back to reality tomorrow.

Chapter Eighteen

Annie had her head bent over her desk, trying to clear her paperwork before the long New Year's weekend. That was the problem with taking a few days off for Christmas: the work just piled up and had to be done anyway.

Oliver had called her the previous day to see if she would be interested in going out for dinner, but Annie had begged off, blaming an overload of work. They made small talk for a few minutes before Annie said she had to get back to work. She didn't ask him when he was heading back to England, because she already knew. Carol had told her that he was due back by the end of January.

Annie had decided she wouldn't see him again. There was no point to it. Every meeting would not only escalate her feelings but serve to remind her of a lost opportunity. And she didn't want to tell him how she felt, because that could only end in one of two ways. If she told him how she felt and he didn't feel the same way, it would be the worst kind of disappointment. If he did feel the way she did, then he'd be forced to decide whether to stay or to return home, because there was no way she was getting involved in a long-distance relationship. Annie wasn't putting anyone in that position. She was keener to let things play out naturally.

Lenore passed by her open door and Annie called out to her.

"Lenore, when is the book club meeting up again?" she asked.

"Next Tuesday," Lenore replied. "Will you come?"

"I will," Annie said. "Can I bring anything?"

Lenore shrugged. "Sure, we just bring snacks. Whatever you want."

"What time?"

"Eight-ish." Lenore smiled. "I'll see you then."

Annie made a note in her diary. She liked the way the inked note looked: like she had plans. Other than work. She'd done a lot of thinking on the drive back. She wasn't ready to move back home yet. New York needed to be explored, and to do that properly she needed to create a life for herself in the city. Even though Oliver was returning to England, Annie decided she was forging ahead without him. The book club was the first step. Saturday morning, she had plans to check out the Tenement Museum. By herself. She had already purchased her ticket online.

"You're still here, Annie," Carol said from the doorway. Annie looked up to see her friend standing there in her coat and gloves. Annie envied her; it would be a while before she would be able to go home. But work was a good distraction.

"Yes," Annie said with a sigh. "Just trying to catch up. Maybe just another hour."

"I'm glad I ran into you," Carol said, leaning against the doorframe.

Annie tapped her pencil against the desk and stifled a yawn, wishing she could go home as well.

"Do you have any plans for New Year's Eve?" Carol asked.

"I don't know yet," Annie said. She was waffling back and forth between going home to Hope Springs, even though she'd just returned, or having a quiet night in. She'd probably opt for the latter, even though it felt pathetic.

"Why don't you come over to our place? Around ten, after the kids are in bed?" Carol said.

"Oh, I don't know," Annie said. She wasn't in the mood for a crowd of people.

"It'll just be us and you and Oliver," Carol said.

At the mention of Oliver's name, Annie blushed.

"I thought it might be nice if we all got together before Oliver went back to England," Carol said.

"Right," Annie said.

"It's great about his promotion, isn't it? And I suppose he was always going to want to go home at some point."

"It's wonderful," Annie said, with no feeling behind her words.

"Anyway, Oliver told Doug he had a great time at the wedding," Carol said. "He said you have a wonderful family."

"Did he? I'm glad. It was nice; we had a good time."

Carol nodded. "It's a shame it didn't work out between the two of you. I had high hopes for you as a couple. But at least you ended up friends, and that's better than nothing."

"Better than nothing," Annie repeated.

"All right, we'll see you tomorrow night at ten?"

"Sure," Annie said halfheartedly.

"Great! See you then," Carol said. "And you don't have to bring anything."

"Okay."

Carol was gone, and Annie stared at the empty space for a long time before returning to work.

CHAPTER NINETEEN

Oliver took the train up from the city to visit Mr. Hardcastle at his home in Connecticut. From his seat by the window, he stared at the endless blanket of snow that covered everything. It was pretty, and parts of it reminded him of England. Normally the reminder would have made him homesick, but not today. The future—his, specifically—was bright and exciting.

The smooth rocking of the train along the tracks made him drowsy. The last few days had been busy and chaotic. He wished Annie were with him on the train. It turned out Connecticut was a pretty state that warranted further investigation.

Since they parted ways after the holiday, Oliver had not stopped thinking about her. In his mind he'd relived, over and over again, every moment he spent with her over the Christmas holidays and all the plans they'd made. She had consumed his thoughts, and he couldn't wait to see her again. He leaned against the window and sighed.

As they had arranged, Oliver took a cab from the train station out to Mr. Hardcastle's home, arriving in the early afternoon. The house was a Palladian-style mansion at the end of a long drive of towering poplars, now bare in the dull winter sun.

Oliver was surprised when Mr. Hardcastle himself answered the front door. He'd expected to be swept off to a study or library by the hired help.

Mr. Hardcastle pulled his pocket watch from his vest pocket and announced, "Oliver, you're right on time! Good man."

"It was a nice ride up," Oliver said, looking around the place.

"Myra's baking in the kitchen, so we'll head back there. If we behave ourselves, she might let us sample some." Mr. Hardcastle grinned.

Oliver followed his boss to the back of the house.

The kitchen was a large, open space with oak cabinets and granite countertops. A wall of windows overlooked a wooded area whose trees appeared gray and bare against the snow. Mrs. Hardcastle stood at the stove, transferring cookies from a baking tray to a cooling rack.

"Myra, this is Oliver Chesterfield, the young man I was telling you about," Mr. Hardcastle said.

"Nice to meet you," Oliver said.

"My husband speaks highly of you," Myra Hardcastle said. Her husband reached for a cookie from the plate and she playfully slapped his hand away with a laugh. "Stop, you've already had three!"

Oliver smiled as she passed the plate to him. "Oliver, would you like a cookie?" Mr. Hardcastle looked disappointed.

Oliver took one and thanked her.

Myra offered to make tea and coffee, and Oliver's boss indicated that he should take a seat at the kitchen table. Once Myra served the tea and left a plate of cookies in the middle of the table, she removed her apron, hung it on a hook inside a broom closet, and left the room.

Mr. Hardcastle opened the conversation. "Are you excited about returning home to England and opening up that branch office for me?"

Oliver hesitated and looked across at the older man. "That's why I asked for a meeting with you. Unfortunately, I won't be able to take that position after all."

If Mr. Hardcastle was surprised, he didn't show it. His face was devoid of emotion, and not for the first time that day, Oliver wondered if he would end up losing his job by not taking the promotion.

Waiting for his boss to reply, Oliver sipped his tea, finding his mouth had gone dry.

Mr. Hardcastle regarded him with narrowed eyes. "May I ask why?"

Oliver swallowed hard and didn't say anything at first.

The elderly man leaned back in his chair and asked, "Would your decision have anything to do with a certain young lady?"

Oliver looked at the old man. His face was full of kindness.

"It has everything to do with her," Oliver admitted.

Mr. Hardcastle nodded. "It's as I thought," he said with a sigh. "I'm disappointed of course, as I have big plans for you, but I understand."

"You do?" Oliver asked, unable to hide his disbelief.

"I do," Mr. Hardcastle repeated. "Your family and your relationships should always come before your job."

Relief flooded through Oliver.

"When I was seventy, I was still working sixty hours a week. Myra became very sick," Mr. Hardcastle told him. His face contorted in pain at the memory of it. "I'd still be working if it hadn't happened. But her illness made me realize the value of things and what was important to me."

"Thank you for being so understanding," Oliver said.

The elderly man waved him off with a smile. "Don't worry about it. I'm impressed with your work ethic and your productivity. Would you consider a partnership?"

Oliver smiled and reached for another cookie. "I would."

Oliver had a hard time locating a parking space near Doug and Carol's brownstone and ended up parking his car four blocks away.

The sidewalks were wet but clear, and windows were still filled with decorated Christmas trees and twinkling lights. He loved this time of the year. Heading toward the new year, so full of hope.

An elderly couple passed him. Their arms were linked together, and they acknowledged Oliver with a smile and a nod.

He ran the last block, anxious to see Annie and tell her his news, and by the time he arrived at Doug and Carol's, he was out of breath. Before he rang the bell, he took in some deep breaths. He could barely wait for them to answer the door, so eager was he to see Annie.

It was almost ten-thirty. He'd been late getting back to the city, as Myra Hardcastle had invited him to stay for dinner after he'd spent an enjoyable afternoon with his boss.

Carol answered the door and Oliver stepped into the foyer and kissed her on her cheek, wishing her a Happy New Year.

"Unfortunately, it's just the three of us," Carol said.

Oliver was in the middle of removing his coat. "Where's Annie?"

Carol shook her head, taking his coat from him. "She called earlier and said she thought she might be coming down with something and wouldn't be able to make it tonight."

Disappointment engulfed Oliver. The one thing he'd been looking forward to that evening was seeing Annie. It had been the only thing. And now she wasn't there.

For the next hour, Oliver went through the motions of being a good guest. He ate and drank everything they offered. They spoke about work and when the subject of his moving to England came up, he was vague with his replies. He'd wanted to share his news with Annie first. Finally, when he could no longer stand it, he stood up and bid them good night.

"But you've only got a half-hour before midnight," Doug protested. "You might as well stay."

"Uh, I . . ." Oliver stammered. How would he tell them he was leaving to go see Annie?

Carol raised an eyebrow. "Unless of course, you're not going home. Do you have another stop to make?"

Oliver nodded, relieved that he didn't have to explain himself. Doug had a look of confusion on his face.

"Where else are you going?"

Carol rolled her eyes. "I'll tell you later, Doug." She jumped up from her seat, got Oliver's coat out of the closet, and handed it to him. "You can make it there in plenty of time to wish her a Happy New Year in person."

"Thanks, Carol." Oliver smiled.

"I'm still lost," Doug said.

Carol turned to him and said pointedly, "He's going to see Annie."

"Ohhh," Doug said with a small nod.

CHAPTER TWENTY

Outside the window of Annie's apartment, it had started to snow. Big, fat flakes cascaded softly to the ground. Annie was curled up on her sofa with all the lights off. She was bathed in the blue illumination from the television screen. At the last minute, she had begged off going over to Carol and Doug's for New Year's Eve. Lied and told them she was coming down with something. Well, it was a half-truth. She was coming down with something: a broken heart. She just couldn't face Oliver. His move home would be the talk of the evening, and she couldn't plaster on a fake smile and be encouraging, not when all her hopes and dreams had been dashed. Better just to stay home and watch old black-and-white movies. She'd ordered *Mrs. Miniver* and was halfway through it. Hungry, she rooted around her kitchen, glad she'd gone grocery shopping after visiting the Tenement

Museum. She'd enjoyed the museum thoroughly and had decided that the following weekend would be spent at a gallery dedicated to German and Austrian art. After much internal debate between popcorn and Christmas cookies, she opted for a bowl of popcorn.

Her phone had been blowing up with texts all evening. First, she'd texted each member of her family to wish them a Happy New Year. Then she texted Rachel to invite her to come up one Saturday so they could spend the day together. Her sister's response had been enthusiastic, and she began spitballing ideas of what she'd like to do. Annie got a text from Violet and responded with an invitation for her young cousin to come up for the weekend on her midterm break in February. Violet's responding text was full of emojis.

Earlier in the day, when she'd been at the museum, she'd received a text from Oliver, stating he was looking forward to seeing her and that he had some news he couldn't wait to share. Annie didn't think she could take any more of Oliver's good news. She'd responded with a generic Happy New Year and said nothing more.

At eleven-thirty, the movie finished and Annie switched over to the live coverage from Times Square. She went into the bathroom to apply the mud mask from the skincare gift set she'd received from Rachel, thinking she'd watch the ball drop and then go to bed. She returned to her sofa and watched the snow falling outside her darkened apartment. She decided on one more resolution for the new year: she was going to get a cat. She wanted some company, and a cat wouldn't move to England on her. Or at least, she hoped not.

The buzzer to her apartment rang, startling her. Who would be turning up this late at night? She ran over to the window overlooking the front stoop. She'd recognize that mop of hair anywhere.

"Oliver?" she whispered. What was he doing there? She put her hand on her face as she remembered the mud mask, trying not to panic. She started for the door, stubbed her toe on the leg of the coffee table and half-hopped, half-ran the rest of the way.

She pressed the intercom button.

"Hello?" Her voice sounded tight, because the mud mask had dried like cement on her face.

"Annie?"

"Oliver?"

"Yes," he said. "May I come up?"

Annie hesitated. She looked down at her brand-new Christmas pajamas and her big, fluffy robe and groaned inwardly. "Um, sure."

She pressed the button allowing him entrance. Then, leaving the door to her apartment ajar, she ran to the bathroom, ran a washcloth under the hot water tap, and began scrubbing off the mask. She retied the sash around her bathrobe and ran her hands through her hair. She swallowed hard.

"Annie? Annie?" Oliver called from the kitchen.

"I'm here," she said, turning off the bathroom light and heading toward the kitchen.

He wore a sport jacket over a V-neck sweater and a pair of jeans. Annie drew in a deep breath and held it.

"Carol said you were sick. I thought I'd check on you and make sure you're all right."

Annie had not wanted to cause any trouble. "I think I'm coming down with something," she corrected.

"I was looking forward to seeing you tonight," Oliver said.

Annie didn't know what to say to that. She looked away, embarrassed at being in her bathrobe. Embarrassed that she most likely still had bits of mud on her face. Embarrassed that he had come all this way to see her, that she had a huge crush on him, and that she wasn't in the same league as him.

"I wasn't up for it," Annie said.

"We could have used a fourth person," Oliver said with a grin. "We felt like a three-legged chair."

Annie smiled; she couldn't help herself.

Oliver paused and said softly, "It just wasn't the same without you."

"Can I take your jacket? Would you like something to drink?" She didn't know what to do with him. It almost hurt to be so near him and not be able to reach out and touch him.

Oliver removed his jacket and hung it neatly over a chair.

"I don't have any celebratory drinks, but I think I have a bottle of wine somewhere," Annie said, glancing around her kitchen. It was a bottle of wine she'd been given last Christmas. She tried to think where she'd last seen it, and she turned with the intent to locate it. It seemed imperative. And it would occupy her while Oliver stood in the middle of her home.

"Annie—"

Turning her attention back to Oliver, she said, "Are you all packed? Ready to go home? When do you leave?"

"That's what I wanted to tell you," he said. "What I wanted to talk to you about."

"Let me see if I can find that wine," she said.

She hoped he wouldn't suggest a long-distance relationship. She caught herself. She certainly was getting ahead of herself. Maybe he was just there to see if she wanted to buy his television or something.

A riot of emotions played out across his face. "Annie, wait a minute. Leave the wine and talk to me for a minute."

"Okay," she said.

"I went to see Mr. Hardcastle today," he started.

"Should we sit down?" she asked, looking around.

Oliver laughed. "No. Hear me out. Would you let me say what I've come here to say?"

She didn't want to hear him out. She didn't want to hear how he was moving on with his life and how there was no room for her. She didn't want to hear how another man was traveling to another part of the world without her.

"Annie," he started again, his voice barely above a whisper.

"Finalizing details? Going over your new remit?" she asked.

Oliver laughed. "One thing I know about you, Annie Beasley, is that when you get nervous you start talking. A lot."

Annie didn't say anything. She pressed her lips together, wishing she weren't so predictable.

"I told Mr. Hardcastle that I couldn't take the job in England," Oliver said, his eyes never leaving her face.

"You can't?" she asked, confused.

"No, Annie, I can't," he said.

"Why not?" Her heart might have skipped a beat; it might have even stopped.

"I'm not ready to leave New York," Oliver said.

Annie had hoped it was she and not the city that had held him back. "No, of course not. You only just got here. You'll need to see more of the city. If you go back now, you might never get to know it as you should."

Oliver steepled his fingers, put them up to his face, and let out a sigh of frustration. "I'm not getting my point across very well. I'm struggling here, Annie."

She didn't know what to say. Her mouth opened slightly but no words came out. No words of reassurance or encouragement.

Oliver's expression changed, and he closed the gap between them and placed his hands on the sides of her face. "It's you. You're the reason I can't leave. You're the reason I don't want to leave. I thought a promotion was what I wanted. It is what I want. Just not like this. I keep thinking back to Christmas night and all those things we said."

Annie nodded and her eyes welled with tears. She'd lost count of how many times she'd thought of those things. All those promises. All those plans.

"Please don't cry," he pleaded. "I want all those things." He paused as he searched her face. "And I want them with you."

He looked intently at her and Annie hoped he would kiss her. She wondered if she closed her eyes if he would.

"I was excited when he offered me the job, but the more I thought about it, the more I realized it wasn't what I truly wanted," Oliver said. "I kept coming back to our conversation on Christmas night and all the things we talked about doing. And I thought, if I was in England, I'd miss all that. And it's not the activities. It's you, Annie. If you wanted to sit on the sofa for six months and watch television, I'd want that too." He hesitated, looked away, and added, "Just to be with you."

Annie blinked, hardly able to comprehend what he was saying. Unable to believe it. "Was Mr. Hardcastle angry?"

Oliver shook his head and smiled. "I was honest with him. I told him I couldn't leave you."

"And he was okay with that?" Annie asked.

Oliver laughed. "Yes, he said if it were up to him, he'd pick you over a job, too."

Annie blushed.

"Do you know after I first met you, I used to look for you in the elevator and the lobby of our building?" he said, laughing.

"You did?" Annie asked in disbelief. "Why?"

"I just wanted a glimpse of you. I know we got off to a bad start, but I had hoped we could start over."

"Oh, Oliver," she said, lowering her head.

He gently lifted her chin so she was facing him.

"And if I'm honest, I dared to hope . . . to hope that maybe our friendship might develop into something more. It was all I thought about Christmas night," he said. "It was all I've thought about since."

Annie placed her hands over his.

He leaned in. This kiss was going to be slow, expected. Welcome. Not a kiss by surprise like the one underneath the mistletoe at the kitchen sink in her parents' house. Annie's head spun. His hands moved from her face to pull her into an embrace. Annie wrapped her arms around his neck and pulled him down to her. In the background, on the television, Annie could hear the sounds of fireworks and shouts and choruses of "Happy New Year." And yes, Annie thought, it was a new year. And she was happy.

One year later...

"Don't be nervous, darling," Oliver said as he put his arm around Annie and pulled her close, kissing the top of her head. They sat in the back of a black taxi, having arrived in the village of Chesterfield by train. They were now en route to Oliver's home.

"Why would you think I'm nervous?" Annie asked, swallowing hard. The diamond ring on her finger sparkled in the bright winter sunshine.

Oliver had brought her to England to meet his parents and the rest of the family. As they'd spent last Christmas together with her family, it was only fair that they'd spend this Christmas with his. From the moment the airline tickets had been purchased, Annie had had many restless nights. She was beyond nervous. Sedation might be required.

Oliver laughed. "Because you talked nonstop and giggled throughout the entire flight."

Annie cringed. "Did I? I'm so sorry."

"There's nothing to be nervous about. They're going to love you just as I do."

Annie wasn't too sure about that. But she was determined to make the best of it. On the flight over, Oliver had told her all the things they would do while they were there, and it sounded like an enviable itinerary. For his sake, she was going to try to curb, or at least hide, her anxiety.

The past year had been a whirlwind. But it had been wonderful. And when Oliver proposed at Thanksgiving dinner at her parents' house, Annie had immediately said yes.

"I should warn you that the jet lag is worse coming from there to here than the other way around," Oliver advised her. He regarded her thoughtfully. "You are so wound up I think you may crash." There was concern written all over his face.

"I'm fine," she said. But she had to admit that even she felt loopy and that she might stagger around everywhere. She hoped his parents wouldn't think she'd been drinking.

"What is it? You've gone very pale," Oliver said worriedly.

Annie leaned against him, loving the solidness of him. "It's nothing." She thought for a moment. "Were you nervous when you met my family?"

Oliver grinned. "It was after I met them that I became nervous."

Annie laughed and playfully punched him on the arm. "Stop it. They love you, you know."

Oliver nodded. "It goes both ways."

They went quiet as they drove through the village. Annie stared out the window, taking everything in. It was a quaint English village, just as she'd pictured it. The road was narrow and winding. The ancient houses and shops with their weathered stone walls and slate roofs were practically on top of the road.

"It's lovely," she murmured.

"You know, it's similar to Hope Springs," Oliver said. "Small village life, great sense of community."

Annie wanted to believe him but she doubted it. They had talked at length about where they would live once they were married and had children. In the past year they had investigated every nook and cranny of New York City, and they had fallen in love with the place, deciding they would make it their home.

They left the village and drove through country roads of fields, pastures, and meadows as far as the eye could see. Annie was mesmerized. Despite it being winter, it looked picture-postcard perfect. The open view was soon obscured by a high stone wall.

Oliver reached over and squeezed Annie's hand. "We're almost there."

Annie's breath caught in her throat as she wondered if the stone wall, which seemed to go on forever, was part of the estate. Her suspicions were confirmed when she spied a large gated entrance and the black cab slowed down. Annie blinked.

As they drove through the gates, Annie's back went rigid as she tried to see the house Oliver grew up in, but it was not in evidence. After a five-minute drive along what she thought had to be the longest driveway in the world, the trees cleared and suddenly, the house was right in front of them.

Annie gasped. It looked as if the entire village could live in it. She counted four floors. There was a grand, circular, gravel-lined driveway out front, in the center of which stood a large fountain with an ascending plume of water.

Annie lowered her voice, and she tried to control the tremor. "Maybe I could stay at a hotel . . ."

Oliver laughed. "No, you stay here. All family stays at the house."

She didn't want to point out to him that this was no house. A mansion? A castle? This was going to be her home for the next two weeks. Suddenly, she was overwhelmed and wondered if it was too late to go home. Her palms were damp and she was grateful that she'd worn gloves.

Oliver helped her out of the back of the cab as the taxi driver removed their luggage from the trunk and deposited it on the front steps.

As Oliver paid the cab driver, the double doors of the manor opened and a slim older man stepped out. Annie looked from him to Oliver, who was putting away his wallet.

Taking a deep breath, Annie approached the man with a smile, steeling her nerves, and extended her hand. "Lord Chesterfield, I'm Annie Beasley. It's nice to meet you."

The man grinned, shaking her hand. "And I'm Hanson, the butler."

Annie went the shade of crimson.

Oliver wrapped an arm around her, kissing her forehead. "Annie, it's all right, don't worry."

Annie hoped that one day they could look back on this and laugh.

"Hanson! How are you?" Oliver said, breaking into a grin. He walked over to him and shook his hand heartily.

"I'm very well, sir." The butler smiled.

As they stepped into the main hall, Annie looked back at their luggage, standing on the steps outside. "Should we bring our bags in?"

"No, they will be brought in and up to our rooms," Oliver replied.

"They're waiting for you in the morning room," Hanson informed them.

"Who's here?" Oliver inquired.

"Everyone," Hanson replied.

Annie tried not to panic. When he'd said "everyone," had he meant the whole village?

They removed their coats and gloves and handed them to Hanson.

"No need to take us down, Hanson, we'll manage it ourselves," Oliver said.

"Very well, Lord Chesterfield," Hanson said.

Oliver took Annie's hand and the two of them proceeded through the main hall, which was two stories in height. Annie didn't know where to look first: at all the portraits stacked on the wall, the huge chandelier suspended from the second floor, or the twelve-foot Christmas tree tucked in the nook of the staircase. Her eyes traveled up the staircase as it wound its way up to the second floor. There was a gallery that wound around the second floor and looked down onto the main foyer.

Down the hall they went, Annie marveling at everything: a display of vases of oriental origin, a suit of armor on display, and more portraits. Violet was right. All the male ancestors had dimples.

Oliver stopped outside a door and Annie could hear voices on the other side, conversations and children laughing and then a dog barking. She began to shake.

"I hate seeing you this upset," Oliver said. Concern transformed his features and Annie relaxed a little. "We can stay at the hotel in town if you like."

Annie searched his face and her mind drifted to last Christmas, when Oliver had stayed with her family. They had only been casual acquaintances and yet he'd fit right in with her family. He'd made the effort. Had been a good sport. Without complaint, he'd put up with numerous relatives, a full house, a gong, clocks, and an endless supply of paper towels.

She reached up and tenderly touched the side of his face. "No, Oliver, I'm going to be fine. And we're going to stay here with your family."

Oliver whispered to her, "The only thing that matters is you and me. That's it. Nothing else." With his hand on the door, he paused and added, "Don't ever forget how much I love you."

He threw the door open wide and Annie took a deep breath, stilled her nerves, and stepped forward into the room, smiling.

ALSO BY MICHELE BROUDER

Also Available in Large Print

The Happy Holidays Series
A Whyte Christmas
This Christmas
A Wish for Christmas
One Kiss for Christmas
A Wedding for Christmas

Escape to Ireland Series
A Match Made in Ireland
Her Fake Irish Husband
Her Irish Inheritance
A Match for the Matchmaker
Home, Sweet Irish Home
An Irish Christmas

Hideaway Bay Series
Coming Home to Hideaway Bay
Meet Me at Sunrise
Moonlight and Promises
When We Were Young

9 781914 476792